ROANOKE

A Novel of the Lost Colony

ROANOKE

A Novel of the Lost Colony

SONIA LEVITIN

New York   Singapore

First Aladdin Paperbacks edition September 2000

Text copyright © 1973 by Sonia Levitin

*Originally published by Antheneum
Books for Young Readers in 1973.*

*Aladdin Paperbacks
An imprint of Simon & Schuster
Children's Publishing Division
1230 Avenue of the Americas
New York, NY 10020*

The text of this book was set in Janson.

Printed and bound in the United States of America

10 9 8 7 6 5 4 3 2 1

*Library of Congress catalog card number: 73-76323
ISBN: 0-689-30114-6 (hc.)*

ISBN: 0-689-83785-2 (Aladdin pbk.)

For Lloyd,
with love

Contents

PART ONE   *I*

PART TWO   *113*

Epiloque   *277*

Part One

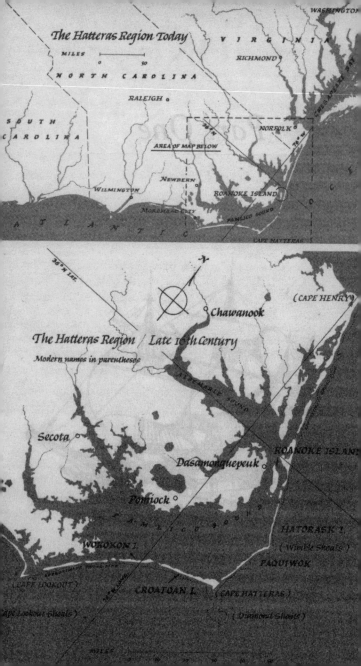

The Hatteras Region Today

MILES
0   90

NORTH CAROLINA

VIRGINIA

WASHINGTON

RICHMOND

RALEIGH

SOUTH CAROLINA

NORFOLK

AREA OF MAP BELOW

NEWBERN

ROANOKE ISLAND

WILMINGTON

MOREHEAD CITY

PAMLICO SOUND

ATLANTIC

CAPE HATTERAS

36° N LAT

Chawanook

The Hatteras Region / Late 16th Century

Modern names in parentheses

ALBEMARLE SOUND

(CAPE HENRY)

Secota

Dasamonquepeuk

ROANOKE ISLAND

Pomiock

PAMLICO SOUND

HATORASK I

(Wimble Shoals)

PAQUIWOK

WOKOKON I

(CAPE LOOKOUT)

CROATOAN I

(CAPE HATTERAS)

Ape Lookout Shoals)

(Diamond Shoals)

MILES

ONE

WHO WILL EVER KNOW the truth of this venture, unless I tell it? I'm called a storyteller, and often I tell the children bits of the past. But just as often I invent tales to amuse them. Someday they will begin to ask questions, and I will owe them true answers.

Sometimes I find myself almost thinking that I've been *here* since the beginning. It would be comfortable to forget the past and the people I've loved and will never see again. But I mustn't let it all go, for I'm the only one left to tell it. And perhaps someday men will come from across the sea looking for answers. Then, if I am gone, they may find this narrative.

My story begins in the year 1587, in my sixteenth year. It begins in the town of Rochester, with the spectacle of a public whipping. I was the victim.

Behind me the crowd jeered and screamed. "Beggar! Idler! Vagabond!"

How long had it gone on? Long enough that there was only one pattern in my brain—the grunt of the constable, the hiss of the whip, then the fire that followed the lash across my back, widening and spreading over me until it swallowed up every other thought. At first I'd been furious, then terrified; all that disappeared into pain.

"Beggar! Idler! Vagabond!"

At first I'd heard their lust, their glee. Then my vision began to blur. A strange, swooning sense of peace washed over me. I had only to give up, to let myself drift and be taken away. . . .

A voice broke through the crowd. "Stop! Listen to me!" Now my senses rushed back, and angrily I pulled against the ropes that bound me.

I realized then that the whip had stopped. Only the voice remained. "Stop it! Listen to me. I know that boy!"

"How dare you!" the constable flung back, panting. "We don't tolerate paupers and beggars here. The law says they shall be whipped, and we're doing our duty."

"He's not a beggar!"

"He's to be an example to others," gasped the constable. "Thieves, beggars. . . ."

I saw the shadow of the whip as he raised it again, then the shadow of the woman as she flung herself at his arm.

"I tell you he's apprenticed!" she cried in the full, passionate voice I knew so well. "His name is William Wythers. He's apprenticed to my husband."

"Ah, then you've come to fetch him back," said the constable, retreating. "Well, that's a different matter. I'll wager his master will want to finish the job himself. Run away, has he? He'll not run away again so soon, I'll wager," he laughed.

I saw the flash of a blade. Then I lurched forward, my head nearly hitting the dust, for the ropes that bound me to the post had been cut in one violent stroke.

Like a dog, I was pulled by the rope and flung toward the woman. "Here's your 'prentice, Mistress . . ."

"Svenson," the woman supplied. "My husband is a carpenter just outside Rochester."

"I'm glad to get this one off my hands," said the constable, wiping his perspiring face with a cloth. "He put up a mean fight." Gingerly he dabbed at the long scratch on his cheek, and I fought the temptation to strike out and plant my knee in his belly.

Someone in the crowd cried out in disappointment, "She's takin' her pretty boy home!" Another answered shrilly, "He'll not be so pretty when his master's had a turn at him!"

"Shall I send a man with you?" asked the constable.

"I'll manage, thank you," replied Mistress Svenson, her bosom heaving. Her voice, her breathing, showed her always at the brink of an outburst, but it never came.

I kept my eyes straight ahead as Mistress Svenson led me to the cart. My hands were still tied together,

5

and I stumbled as the constable pushed and prodded me. Mistress Svenson mounted, the whip firmly in her hand.

"Hold on!" The constable barred the way. "There's still the matter of a fine. Two crowns for vagrancy."

"Very well." She took the coins from the pouch tucked into her bodice. "He won't bother you again," she said, and held her head high as we rode past the scowling mob. Her back remained tensely arched until we were out of the town.

At last she halted the team under a tree and faced me. "How far did you think you would get without identification?" she demanded.

I glanced over the deserted road, then at her. She was strongly built, and I felt sick and weak from lack of food. My body still ached from the whip. And she'd been kind to me in the past. I didn't want to struggle with her. But the thought of being dragged back to Svenson brought another surge of anger.

"I didn't take time to think about identification," I replied bitterly. Concealed under my shirt, I kept trying to work my fingers through the knot. But the rope had been waxed and remained rigid. "My only thought," I added, "was to get away."

It seemed an ideal time for escape. Svenson had been commissioned by a gentleman to build a carved screen. He would never sacrifice such an opportunity to go and search for a missing apprentice. The thought that he'd sent his wife to find me, made me hate him even more.

"You should have been more clever," Mrs. Svenson said coldly, "than to show your face in daylight."

"I walked all night. When morning came, I hid in a shed and fell asleep. Next thing I knew a farmer was standing over me with his pitchfork. His son, the brat, had seen me and called his father."

"And you put up a fair fight," she said, eying the bruise on my chin. She sighed deeply, then said in her heated tone, "I would never have believed it of you, William Wythers! I always thought you were an honorable lad. When other women complained about their apprentices, I could tell them that you, *you* had never stolen from us."

"Stolen!" I cried. "I haven't stolen anything!"

"It only shows that one can never trust. . . ."

"I didn't take anything," I repeated. "I swear, I don't know what you mean."

The lines in her face deepened. Slowly she said, "When my husband saw you had gone, he went to the strongbox. It was wide open. Three gold sovereigns were missing."

My head throbbed with confusion. "You think I took them?"

"Can you deny it?"

"Yes!" I shouted with all the strength I could muster. "If I had been at the strongbox," I demanded, "wouldn't I also have taken my papers? And if you were so sure I was the thief, why didn't you tell the constable back there?"

She paused. "I didn't want to believe it."

"Do you want to search me?" I asked.

She shook her head slowly. "I'm glad I found you, and not Master Svenson," she said. "But he won't give up looking. He has reported you to the sheriff as a thief."

From under the seat she took a stout knife. "Hold out your wrists," she commanded. Then, neatly she sliced the rope. When it was done, she said, "Go quickly. You won't have any more trouble if you keep to the bushes."

I stared at her, and my throat was so dry I could hardly get out the words. "You're not—taking me back?"

"No," she said. "My husband is . . ." she sighed. "He is a hard man. Maybe he doesn't mean to be cruel. But his mood was always best after he'd beaten you."

"It wasn't the beatings, Mistress Svenson," I assured her. "I didn't come to him for gentleness, only to learn the trade."

She nodded. "It was because of the table and the little chests you'd made," she stated. "He wouldn't understand that, even if I told him."

"What will you tell him?" I was suddenly afraid for her.

"Nothing," she replied. "He didn't know I had come to search for you. But where will you go, William?"

"I'll find a place," I said simply. I didn't tell her anything that her husband could later force her to reveal.

"Go then," she said, pressing my hand, "and Godspeed, William."

"One moment, Mistress." I got down from the cart and turned my back to her, taking out the leather purse I wore concealed around my waist. I took out two crowns from the few coins my father had given me long before as a parting gift. I held them out to her, and she protested,

"You'll need it more than I, William."

"No," I said firmly. "I am already indebted to you."

At last she took the money, shaking her head sadly. "You do have a goodly share of pride, haven't you?" Then she swung the cart around and was off, her dark cloak flapping in the wind.

On horseback or by coach the journey to London would have taken less than two hours. But every time I heard the rumble of an approaching coach, I darted behind a bush or a rock. Anyone seeing my torn clothes and battered face would have taken me for a vagabond or a thief and would have used whatever weapon was handy.

It was long past sundown when I reached London, shivering from cold and exhaustion. I had stumbled while crossing a narrow footbridge; my clothes were still damp and covered with mire.

I kept to the darkest streets, turning my face when anyone approached. Without a lantern or any weapon, I knew I was easy prey for the beggars and cutthroats who haunted the city at night.

Several times I had to stop to get my bearings,

then retrace my steps, for a low, clinging fog shrouded the buildings, making them unfamiliar. Then I heard the bells from St. Paul's. The sound brought a surge of relief and new strength to my limbs. I was near my destination.

There was one household in London where I would find refuge, that of Master Taylor, the baker. I had gone there as a child to romp with his sons, Hugh and Clement, and to taste the cakes from his bakeshop.

Before my mother died, Hugh Taylor and I had been taught our letters together at the house of Dame Broody. As she went about her housework, we read aloud to her, usually from the prayer book. Hugh, always bent on mischief, would try his best to make me laugh by twisting his face into strange expressions. He certainly took the dullness out of lessons.

It was Hugh who nearly a year before had sent the message telling me of my father's death, and about Bessie.

"Your sister Elizabeth has come to live with us as our ward, and she is a good companion to my mother, especially since my father has been abroad. If you should ever find yourself in London. . . ."

At last I reached St. Bartholomew's, then turned to Aldersgate Street with its rows of half-timbered houses and shops. Their windows were sealed tight against the night air.

I stood before the darkened old bakeshop, looking up at the rooms above. Between the shutters I saw a faint light. Suddenly I felt overcome by weariness, but I steadied myself against the wall and rapped loudly on the door.

The casement was thrown aside, and a man's head appeared at the window. "Who's there at this hour?" came the booming voice. "The shop's closed."

"It's William Wythers, sir," I shouted up, with a great longing to be inside and safe. A candle was brought to the window, and Master Taylor exclaimed, "William! A moment, lad, I'll come down."

The door was flung open, and Master Taylor, catching a clear sight of me cried, "Good Lord, what's happened? Come in!" I was led up the narrow staircase to the parlor, where Mistress Taylor, seeing me, covered her face in fright.

"William Wythers! You're bleeding!" She flung aside her sewing and rushed to take my arm. "Sit down here by the fire," she urged. "There now, there. You're shivering. Hugh!" she called. "Fetch some ale. Are you hungry, lad? Hugh! Bring some food. It's William Wythers, near collapsed."

They hovered around me while I ate. Mistress Taylor filled my plate again and again, murmuring, "There's plenty, William. Eat slowly, lad. There's plenty."

She was, all at once, dear and familiar to me, just the same as I remembered, although her hair was quite gray. But her black eyes were bright, and her gentle, motherly murmurings made me feel at peace.

Hugh strode about, fetching more bread, poking the fire, tousling the hair of his brother, Robert, a slender serious boy of twelve who sat on a cushion at my feet, staring. Clement, always the quiet one, sat back fingering his beard, simply watching me. All the while Hugh was fetching and bringing me food, he exclaimed over my condition and shot out questions I could not yet answer.

At last I felt restored enough to speak. "Elizabeth," I began, "how is she?"

"Quite well," answered Mistress Taylor. "She speaks of you often. She'll be overjoyed to see you."

"I'll go wake her," said Robert, nearly tripping in his haste, but his mother stopped him.

"William can wait and first compose himself."

"Now tell us," said Master Taylor, settling himself to look at me squarely, "tell us everything. You've been in a fight, that's plain to see."

His voice was firm and robust, as I remembered it, but he too had grayed, and his shoulders were stooped. And strangely, his complexion, once fair as Clement's, had become deeply tanned.

"Did Svenson let you off?" Hugh asked. His pointed beard and long side locks gave him a dashing and distinguished look. His eyes were fiery with life; his very movements seemed to show a craving for action and adventure.

"Did you run away?" Robert asked excitedly. "Did you meet up with bandits?"

"Let William speak!" roared the father. "Sit down, Hugh, and stop that tramping. And Robert, hold your tongue, or you'll be off to bed."

"I did run away from Svenson," I began. "I was caught, beaten...." I told them everything, and before I had finished Mistress Taylor went to fetch a pot of goose grease for my back. "There," she soothed, "this will ease the pain. But the marks of that scoundrel's whip won't fade so soon." She turned to Hugh. "Bring William a shirt of yours. Robert's would never fit. You've nearly grown to manhood," she said to me, smiling.

"So you are sought now as a thief," said Master Taylor with a deep frown. "Why did you leave Svenson? Was he cruel?"

"Cruel? Yes," I murmured, and I desperately wished that I was clever with words, to make Master Taylor understand. I had committed a drastic act in running away. Would Master Taylor think I had been foolish and even perverse?

"I didn't run away because of his beatings," I said earnestly. "I didn't object to doing all the mean and heavy work about the place. I hadn't expected more."

Again I remembered my father's parting words when he apprenticed me. "Work hard, and don't look for luck or favors." It was the last time I ever saw him. Then came the letter, "... a terrible accident ... may the Lord rest his soul...." My father had been crushed to death beneath a crumbling brick wall.

My loneliness then was like a heavy burden. It would overwhelm me in the night or even as I went about my tasks. For I had lived with the hope that, after a year of working with Svenson, my father would release me, take me home and find me a better master.

"Svenson was skillful," I said with bitterness, "skillful at substituting poor or unseasoned wood when he thought he could get by with it. He never let me finish anything, saying that I was not capable. How could I ever get better? I've heard of masters who keep their apprentices chained to them that way, keeping them as servants for years.

"But at night," I continued, "I worked alone with scraps. I made several small chests and miniature furniture—for dolls," I said sheepishly. Master Taylor only nodded.

Once I had begun to lose myself in my carvings, my loneliness had lifted. But I longed to try my hand at something real.

"At last Svenson let me make a small table," I continued. "He was too busy with larger assignments. It was to be an ordinary table for an ordinary man, and Svenson ordered me to use the worst scraps for it. I was to work on it between my regular chores, but there wasn't time, so I worked at night."

Sometimes I had worked until dawn, forgetting everything in my complete absorption. I carved the legs in delicate detail. I sanded and rubbed the wood until it gleamed like marble.

"I kept the table by my bed," I continued, "and sometimes Svenson came to look, saying only that I was too slow. His wife saw it, and," I said simply, "she liked it."

I didn't repeat Mistress Svenson's words, or try to describe her look when she said them, "You've a gift in your hands, William, and a heart within you. I see both in your work."

Hugh broke in to ask, "Did the customer like it?"

I nodded. "When it was finished, Svenson only grunted. Then the customer came for the table. Oh, he liked it! He shook Svenson's hand again and again, said it was a finer thing than he had expected. I was sweeping up, and Svenson caught sight of me. He ordered me away like a cur. He shouted that I had no business in the shop while a 'gentleman' was present, that I was a loafer, a ne'er-do-well. When the man left he began to curse me in a furious rage. He found the small chests and things I'd made and threw them into the fire."

I felt exhausted from telling this, from the old anger that flared up again within me.

"It's a hard thing to bear," Master Taylor said at last.

"I only wanted the credit due me!" I exclaimed. "Only to hear my name spoken!"

"A hard thing," Taylor mused, "for a master when his pupil learns too quickly and too well."

I was stunned. "You mean, he was angry because I had done well?"

"It doesn't matter now," Master Taylor said. "You ran away to protect your honor, and now you are wanted as a thief."

"But he would be worse off," Hugh said, "if he'd stayed. Svenson would still have blamed him for the theft."

"That's true," I nodded. "If I'd stayed, I'd be in prison now."

"You might have explained," Master Taylor pointed out.

"Not to Svenson," I replied. "He'd never have believed me, and he has some say with the sheriff. It happens that I do have some money my father left me. But I have no proof of where I got it, except my word, and that doesn't count for much. But that Svenson should have been robbed on the very night of my escape! Luck," I said sadly, "hasn't been on my side."

"The ways of the Lord are strange," whispered Mistress Taylor. "What's to become of you, William?" she sighed.

In planning my escape, I had thought to apprentice myself to another carpenter somewhere. But now all that was changed. My few coins would soon be gone. For a pauper the only destination was the almshouse—for a thief, the prison. Now there was only one route I could take. It would save my honor and even my life.

"I have planned," I said, "to go to sea." And, having spoken the words aloud, I knew that there was no turning back.

TWO

MY ANNOUNCEMENT was greeted with deadly silence. Master Taylor and his sons exchanged glances.

"It's late," said Master Taylor brusquely. He took the prayer book from its table, then bowed his head.

"Lord, help us to turn aside from desires for worldly gain, and to turn our thoughts instead to Thy service. . . ."

We prayed in unison, "There is one invisible God, creating Himself and all creatures. He is of the highest good. . . ."

They took up their candles, and Mistress Taylor said, "Come, William. You'll want to see your sister before you sleep."

I followed her up the steep, winding stair to the turret rooms. It was a long time since anyone had lighted my way.

Mistress Taylor opened the door to a closet-sized room, where Elizabeth lay asleep on a great four-poster. She looked small and frail under the heavy featherbed. Her blond hair was strewn on the pillow, her hands clasped beneath her chin.

"She's a good child," whispered Mistress Taylor, "and she looks so like your dear mother."

"Yes," I whispered. "Poor Bessie—she hasn't even the memory."

She had been only two, unable to understand about plague and death. "Mama's gone to Heaven," we told her, and she didn't even cry. But later in the night, when she called out and her mama did not come—I had to hold her all through the night, to hear her sobbing, until at last she slept from sheer exhaustion.

"We won't wake her," whispered Mistress Taylor. "She's had a full day with Master Taylor in the bakery, then working over her mending."

But in that moment Bessie's eyes opened, and she sat bolt upright. "William! William! Is it really you?"

She flung her arms around my neck, and I held her, laughing, although her hands on my back made the flesh burn.

"Yes, really, I'm here, Bessie."

"Don't leave me ever again, William," she implored, and her enormous dark eyes filled with tears. "Every night I've prayed that you would come."

"Then your prayer has been answered," I said,

smiling. "Don't cry. You're so big now—eight years old," I said, though I knew better.

"I'm nine, William," she argued, forgetting her tears.

"Oh, yes, of course," I nodded. "And Mistress Taylor tells me you're getting on well. Go back to sleep now." I kissed her cheek, and as I left her I thought once more of my decision, "I'm going to sea."

* * *

"Are you really going to sea?" Young Robert bounced on the large canopied bed we were to share. "Father's been to sea. He's even been to Virginia. He spent a whole year there and nearly starved to death, until Sir Francis Drake came to the rescue!"

"Virginia!" I exclaimed, scarcely knowing whether or not to believe the boy. "Isn't that someplace in the Indies?"

Hugh threw back his head in a roar of laughter. "You've been in the country too long, William! Virginia is in the New World! Sir Walter Raleigh sent an expedition there last year. 'Twas for this he was knighted, you know."

"I'd heard something of the sort," I murmured vaguely.

"My father went along as baker to the company," said Hugh. "Didn't you find him changed?" He sat down beside me and began to polish his sword.

"I did. I had wondered about it. He is darkly tanned."

"And filled with bold tales of treasure," said Hugh, "and of battles against the savages. It was a fine adventure." His eyes gleamed. "Virginia—doesn't the very sound of it stir your blood? We're going, Clement and I."

I stared at him, almost laughing aloud in my utter confusion. "You're not serious!" I protested.

Now Clement came from behind his bed curtains, nodding gravely. "We're to sail in a fortnight," he said.

"How many of you? What will you do there? *Why?*" I had heard talk of exploration, wild rumors I thought, yet here beside me were Hugh and Clement Taylor, speaking seriously of going to a new and savage land called Virginia.

"About a hundred of us," Clement replied. "We're going to plant a colony."

"You mean you're going to stay?" I gasped.

"Oh, we might return to England some day to visit," Hugh said with a flourish. "Colonies are just beginning, William. There will be others, later, to follow us."

"You *are* in earnest about this," I said in awe.

"Indeed we are," said Clement, looking sober as a priest in his white nightshirt. "The Queen herself considers it a matter of great importance."

"She gave her name to the new land," Hugh added. "Sir Walter Raleigh stakes his reputation, not to speak of his fortune, on this venture. Of course, Raleigh wanted to go himself, to be governor of the colony. But the Queen won't part with him," he said with a knowing wink.

I felt dizzy and awed at hearing the names of persons of such power spoken so glibly. For the first time in my life I had the sense that these were real people. Strange as it seems, I had never thought of them as flesh-and-blood creatures. It all had a powerful effect on me.

"There is treasure, you say," I murmured, "and land, ripe for the taking?"

"Not on Roanoke, where Lane settled," Hugh explained. "But the natives told of pearls and gold to be found at the mouth of a great river called Chesapeake. We plan to settle at Chesapeake."

"Raleigh, then, believes there is treasure?" I asked, taking the courtier's name boldly.

"Who can know what Raleigh believes," Hugh shrugged. "We're to settle at Chesapeake because, well, there were problems on Roanoke with the savages."

"Problems!" Clement exclaimed in a rare outburst. "Problems, he says, when what he means is butchery!"

"Well, now Clement," said Hugh, "we don't know the whole story. Father wasn't actually in on the skirmishes." Hugh turned to me and, lowering his voice said, "My father says Governor Lane was a fool. He stormed all over the countryside seeking treasure and warring against the savages, instead of planting his fort. So when winter came, they nearly starved."

"Tell it!" Robert breathed. "Tell it again—about the savages in England."

"Savages in England!" I exclaimed.

Hugh nodded. "It's true. A year before Governor Lane's colony, Raleigh sent an expedition to the New World to see whether it would be profitable to plant a colony there. The explorers said it was a fine land, and the savages most friendly. They brought back tokens from the New World," he added, grinning. "Among them were two living savages called Manteo and Wanchese."

"Savages in England!" I repeated, dazed.

Hugh nodded. "They stayed in the palace for nearly a year. They were returned to Virginia with Governor Lane's colony. As soon as they were back on their native soil, that one called Wanchese began to stir up the other savages against our men."

"Why?" I asked, but Hugh only shrugged.

"He had reason enough," Clement said. "Captain Grenville who'd brought them all to Roanoke, burned down a whole native village because one of the savages had stolen a silver cup."

"There were several skirmishes," Hugh went on, "and treachery on both sides. Some heads were cut off," he said, squinting at his sword. "Unfortunately one of the heads belonged to a chief called Pemisipan. That is why we won't go back to settle on Roanoke."

"But if that Chief, Pemisipan's dead . . ." I began.

"He had friends and followers," said Hugh. "Wanchese was one of them. None of that really matters now. We'll start afresh at Chesapeake."

"But what will you *do* there?" I asked again,

unable to grasp it all. The world was moving at a frenzied pace, and I had been standing still.

"Do?" Hugh echoed. "We'll explore, we'll claim the land, hold it, defend it."

"Not I," said Clément. "I'll be a baker."

Hugh laughed. "Oh, Clement, you'll never change. If you'd seen a campaign or two. . . ."

"Even soldiers have to eat," Clement retorted, "and I'd rather fill men's bellies than slit them open."

I learned that Hugh had been to Ireland on a campaign just this past spring, while Clement had remained behind to work with his father. Of course, joining the Roanoke venture had been Hugh's idea, and his excitement was contagious. I could feel it affecting me. I could see it affecting Robert.

"The New World is rich and vast beyond imagining," Hugh said, caressing his sword. "Everywhere there is land and treasure ripe for the taking."

"Will you become a gentleman, even a squire?" Robert asked, his face flushed with excitement and longing.

"I'll wager the Queen will show her gratitude," Hugh said coolly.

Young Robert grasped his brother's arm. His eyes burned with tears of envy and yearning. "Ah, I want to go too! I would give anything! Can't you beg mother to let me go?"

Hugh put him off gently, shaking his head. "We've had enough talk for one night," he said, blowing out the candle.

In the silence I heard Robert's quick, tormented breathing and he lay tensely beside me. After a time he whispered, close to my ear, "Why don't you go too?"

I pretended to be asleep. My thoughts were so deep, so terrifyingly bold. I didn't really want to be a seaman. I'd seen mariners in the streets and pubs. You could always tell a seaman by the brooding, haunted look on his face.

How could a man make his mark in the world? He could become an adventurer, like Drake and Hawkins, but there were very few of these. It was land that made a gentleman. With land of my own, and a bit of gold, I could do anything I wanted.

My father had never even dared to dream of such things. And my gentle mother would have been horrified at such a show of vanity. "Vanity is a sin, my child," she had often told me. "We must learn to be content with our lot."

If my father had lived, I would have worked beside him. I would have been satisfied to earn the title, "Master." Now all that was impossible.

Surely it was a good omen that I had left Svenson when I did. Suddenly a whole world lay before me— the New World. Virginia.

I'd heard rumors about it, wild fancies, I'd thought. One time an old seaman had come into Svenson's. I'd heard him talking. He had been told by a friend, who'd been told by another, that there was a place in the New World with mines so rich that they could be approached only at night. The diamonds glared so brightly in the sunlight that a man could become blinded! And there was a sea so laden with pearls that the tide tossed them up onto the shore, and they lay there, as large as peas.

I stayed awake long after the others were asleep, my blood throbbing with excitement. I made my decision; I would go to the New World.

At last I slept, and in my troubled dreams I heard Bessie's voice pleading, "William, don't go." And I heard my own firm reply, "I'm going. I must."

* * *

I awakened to the sounds of late morning, the rumble of coaches, the snap of a whip, the clap of high-heeled boots on cobblestones. I heard the tinkle of the brass bell from Master Taylor's shop below. Now the fragrance of fresh bread aroused me fully. I pulled on my clothes to rush down to where Master Taylor stood, paddle in hand, taking loaves from the large black oven.

"You look well restored," he greeted me cheerfully. He handed me part of a small fresh loaf, beckoned me to a stool, and poured out a cup of mead.

"Where is everyone?" I asked.

"Robert's minding the shop," Taylor replied, kneading and prodding a large ball of dough as he spoke. "My wife took Bessie to market, and Hugh and Clement are gone about their business."

"A bold business, I hear," said I, having no patience for idle talk. "They told me about their voyage to Virginia." My heart was pounding fiercely, but I looked Taylor straight in the eyes and declared, "I want to go, too."

"I thought you meant to go to sea," he remarked, still working.

"It seemed my only choice before I heard of this voyage," I replied.

"There is another choice, William. Mistress Taylor and I spoke about it last night. You are welcome to stay here as long as you like. This affair with Svenson. . . ."

"I must go, sir, while I have the chance," I said firmly, "though I thank you."

"The boys have been filling your ears with talk of treasure, no doubt," he said, shaking his head. "I've been there, and I saw none at all. Do you expect to find life easier in an untamed land, among savages?"

"No, sir. But I want to make a place for myself—and for Bessie. I want to care for her as soon as I am able. You have been generous. . . ."

"Your father would have done the same for a child of mine," Taylor replied brusquely.

"Tell me about the New World," I begged, but Master Taylor only sighed.

"What can I tell you? I can say that it is vast. But how can you imagine it? Can you picture a land where no civilized man has lived? Look about you! The streets, the houses, the shops, the crowds of people, horses hitched outside the tavern, church bells from St. Paul's—can you imagine it all gone? Can you imagine wilderness?"

"No. I must see it for myself."

"I have told this to Hugh and Clement," the

baker sighed. "But they are grown men, or nearly so, and headstrong. Well, perhaps for them. . . ." he said vaguely, looking to a distance, "I cannot stop them."

"I intend to go, Master Taylor," I said earnestly. "Whom must I ask?"

"John White is to be Governor of the colony," Taylor replied. "He may question you closely. But he's a good man, and fair."

I would have set out that minute, but Master Taylor stopped me, laughing. "Hold on, lad! You can't approach the Governor of Virginia looking like a ragamuffin."

Together we looked in Hugh's cupboard and found a presentable pair of hose, a hat with a bold yellow feather, and a soft dark blue cloak.

I waited while Master Taylor penned a letter. "Give this to John White," he said, adding, "I hope he hasn't already left."

"If he's gone," I asked, "is there another person I can see?"

"You'd have to take your chances, make your way to the port at Plymouth. Or would you interview Sir Walter Raleigh himself?"

I laughed. "Yes, I would, if need be."

My spirits soared as I waved goodbye, bound for my first taste of adventure.

THREE

IT WAS NOT FAR to Cannon Street. But as I walked down toward the Thames I seemed to be reliving all the years of my childhood. Every turn held memories. I had walked here often with my father. I passed the merchant's stalls, where chickens hung by their necks. Housewives crowded around, prodding and pinching before they chose. The strong aroma of spices—cinnamon, pepper, curry and clove—brought vivid images to my mind. How often my father had spoken to me of those distant lands where spices grew—Cathay, India, Persia. Now I realized that I had always held a yearning to see such wonders. Now all of them were combined for me in the single word *Virginia*.

I walked quickly past the churchyard of St. Paul's, whispering a hasty prayer under my breath. I did not like to think about the dead. A hint of the old ache came over me.

But when I saw the masts of ships crowded together in the harbor all that was forgotten. I could hear the lusty shouts of sailors. It was a fine day. A fresh breeze had blown aside the night fog, leaving the air crisp and clear. I squared my shoulders, lifted my head, and pulled Hugh's cloak tightly around me. The cloak was a bit long, but it served to cover my worn breeches, and the soft blue velvet gave me a feeling of wealth.

If I had ever owned such a fine cloak, I couldn't remember it. There were good times before my mother died—money for schooling, plenty of food and a bit of sport on occasion. After Mother died, everything changed. My father had to hire a woman to care for Bessie and me, and I was too small to bring in any money. Then came my father's accident, which left him crippled in one leg. He had been used to working in high places, mending walls, building towers. He lost his nerve after Mother was gone, and one day he fell. For a long while he couldn't work at all, so he went into debt. Even after I was apprenticed, and there was one less mouth to feed at home, I know it was hard. He died, still indebted, still ignoring the bad omen of the accident. He had never left off attempting to get his nerve back on the high places. He was stubborn that way.

It does seem that some men are always struggling, while others seem fated to succeed. Take Master Taylor, no better man than my father—but with three sons to help, and with important friends to speak on his behalf, he owns one of the best shops in London, and he wants for nothing.

Well, enough of the past! I decided. What might my father have thought to see me now, bound for this meeting with Master John White, and dressed almost like a gentleman's son!

A beggar boy was rolling marbles in the dust. He looked up as I approached, and I asked him, "Do you know Master White's house?"

Wordlessly the boy pointed a grimy finger, then returned to his game.

For a full minute I stood before the door, summoning my courage. I would have to reveal my history to John White. He would have every right to send me away, to call me impudent. "The New World, for the likes of you?" I could hear him mocking me. "Do you have papers? Do you have money? Do you have *anything* to recommend you?"

"A letter from Master John Taylor!" I cried out, so engrossed in my play acting that I didn't realize I had knocked and that the door had been flung open. And I stood there like an idiot, shouting, "A letter from Master John Taylor!"

It was a girl—no, a young woman—and my quick glance took in the sweep of her reddish hair, the deep cut of her bodice, and her look of mingled amusement and disdain.

"Well then, I'll take it to him," she said.

"No, no!" I cried out. "I must see him myself." For an instant she simply stared at me, no doubt thinking I was deranged and perhaps dangerous. I realized with overwhelming shame that I had neither taken off my cap nor bowed—that indeed, I had not made a single civil gesture.

"You must see him?" she repeated with a smile that sent me into further waves of confusion. "Very well then. Come *in*."

I stepped inside onto the richly patterned carpet. She waited for me to speak, then prompted, "I must tell him your name."

"William Wythers," I said clearly, resolving to stand up straight and to keep my wits about me. Now I took off my cap and bowed slightly from the waist.

"I am John White's daughter," she responded, "Mistress Elinor Dare." She motioned for me to follow her through the hallway. At the door to another room she paused and said, "Father, there's a *boy* to see you."

The word stung, and I could feel my cheeks redden. Well then, I had not exactly behaved like a man, either! I took a deep breath, preparing to address John White himself.

"Send him in," came a voice from afar.

I had imagined John White to be dressed like a courtier, and to greet me in the stiff, brusque manner of a military man. So I was surprised to behold a man dressed in a simple smock and mild in his movements. He turned to smile at his daughter, and that same smile extended to me.

"Sit down, William Wythers," he said in soft Irish accents, when his daughter had given my name. "Let me take your cloak."

I didn't want to part with the cloak. It seemed to give me courage, and it covered my worn breeches. But I had no choice, for a fire blazed on the hearth.

"Well, now," he said, seeing my letter, "you have a message for me?"

"Yes, sir," I said briskly, handing him the letter.

While he read it, I glanced over his desk, littered with papers. A small table held a clutter of paints and brushes. Boldly colored pictures were propped against the walls, and now I noticed that John White's fingers were stained with pigments. This, then, was his studio, and it came as a bit of a shock that he was an artist. I could not imagine why an *artist* had been appointed governor of a colony.

John White put down the letter and faced me. "Have you read this?" he asked.

"No, sir."

"It says that you are an honorable lad and skilled in carpentry. You wish to join the colonists to Virginia."

"Yes, sir," I said ardently.

"Are you quite alone in the world?"

"My mother died when I was nine. My father was killed nearly a year ago. I have only my little sister. She is a ward to Master Taylor."

"And what would you do in the New World?" Governor White questioned.

"I'd work. I would do whatever is required of me."

"And your friends, Hugh and Clement Taylor—

do you plan to travel under their protection?" His gaze was intense.

"No," I said instantly. "It was through them that I learned about this voyage. But I don't expect any man to be responsible for me."

"Well spoken," he said with a smile. "As to your past—Master Taylor mentions that you were involved in some unpleasant incident."

I opened my mouth to reply, but instantly he silenced me with his uplifted hand. "I don't have to know the details. Master Taylor will vouch for you, and that's enough. In the New World a man can make a new beginning. None will ask questions." Then he asked, "How old are you, William?"

"Sixteen, sir."

"You realize," he said emphatically, "that if you commit yourself to this venture, you are bound to remain in Virginia. If you have any thoughts of first judging the country, I must warn you that from Virginia there is no other place to go."

"I understand," I murmured. Then I ventured to ask, "You yourself have been to Virginia?"

"I have. I spent nearly a year on Roanoke Island serving as artist to Governor Lane's colony. We left in distress," he said, frowning, and I recalled Clement's bitter accusations against Governor Lane.

"We were not able to wait for our supply ships to come," White continued. "Captain Grenville, who brought us to Virginia, had promised to return with supplies the following spring. We waited until June. Fortunately—or unfortunately," White said with a rueful smile, "Sir Francis Drake had decided to pay us a visit. He offered us a ship and supplies to carry us back to England. We accepted."

"And Captain Grenville?" I asked.

"Captain Grenville arrived with the promised supplies two weeks later," Governor White told me. "He searched for us. Finding us gone, he left fifteen of his men on Roanoke to hold England's claim to the land. You must know that the Spaniards, too, would like to get their hands on the area."

I nodded, feeling light-headed at the realization that I was sitting in Master White's own parlor, and that he was speaking to me as a colleague. It must mean—could it possibly mean that he had already decided to accept me?

"Our first task," Governor White continued, "will be to rescue the men left by Captain Grenville. Then we shall proceed to Chesapeake. I have not seen Chesapeake. But if it is anything like Roanoke, I can tell you honestly, it is a fine land, a goodly land. This time," he said, his eyes flaming, "it will be different. We'll settle, and we will stay. With women along, and young people like yourself. . . ."

"Women!" I exclaimed, before I realized that he had also included me.

"Of course." The Governor chuckled. "Did you think we could plant a permanent colony without women? My own daughter is going. Her husband, Ananais Dare, will be in charge of building our fort at Chesapeake. He's gone ahead to Portsmouth to lay in supplies."

John White took up his quill and wrote several words. Then he looked up at me and said briskly, "You'll be working with Master Dare. By the way, have you had schooling?"

"I know how to read and write," I said with some pride.

"Good. Of course, you will be expected to work on shipboard to help pay for your passage. For a while you will be indebted to the company."

I summoned my courage and told him, "When we are well settled, sir, I would like to send for my sister, Bessie. She could come with the next group of colonists."

White pursed his lips and nodded slowly. "Would she be willing?" he mused.

"She will come if I tell her," I replied. "I am the head of our household now. I'm the one who should give her a home."

"You've a good deal of pride, haven't you?" White remarked.

I sighed but did not answer. An excess of pride was a sin.

"Well, a bit of pride is needed for any venture," he said smiling. He stood up, indicating that the interview was over. With a wave of his hand he drew me to his paintings and sketches. "These were painted in Virginia," he said. "These are some of the things you will see."

I gazed at them—the paintings of bark huts set in circles, the brown and barely clad savages with strange markings on their bodies, smiling, dancing,

35

eating, hunting. There were birds and fishes and creeping creatures marvelously colored and strange—so strange! I gasped and blurted out, "Oh, if only I could paint!"

John White laughed and laid a hand on my shoulder. "I feel the same," he said. "Perhaps when we're well settled I'll have time."

He led me to the door and said briskly, "You must be prepared to leave in two days. We sail from Portsmouth. I will find a place for you in one of the coaches. Will you see yourself out, William? I have much to do and even the servants . . ." His voice trailed off, and I said,

"Yes, yes," taking up my cloak and hat and making my way through the house. My hand froze on the doorknob, as the sound of a voice, raised high in wailing, came from the adjoining room.

"They'll blame me, both of them! You must tell him, or I will. I've pledged my life to your father's service, and I can't let him be. . . ."

"You'll say nothing, Agnes," came Mistress Dare's voice, cool and firm. "You are in my service now, and if you say one word, I'll. . . ."

Again the servant wailed, "But Mistress, what's to become of it, the little lamb, poor little lost lamb, among the heathen?"

Now Elinor Dare's voice was raised high in anger. "Be done now, or I'll leave you behind, I swear, and what's to become of *you* then?"

I marveled at the strength of that voice in contrast to the gentle, gay tone she'd used before. What could have caused this? Well, it was no business of mine. Noiselessly I closed the door behind me.

Outside, I was struck with the full awareness that from this moment on my life was completely changed. No longer was I William Wythers, apprentice, William Wythers, pauper. I was William Wythers, colonist, part of a company of men and women sent by the Queen herself to do a bolder thing than I had ever dreamed.

* * *

Bessie huddled in a corner of the couch, shivering.

"You can't go," she repeated, her eyes red and heavy lidded from crying.

"Now Bessie," I coaxed, "don't take on. I'll send for you. I told Governor White himself that you are to come."

"You can't go!" she cried.

"I must. Would you rather I went to prison?"

"You'll never get there," she whispered. "I've heard about the black edge of the sea. There are monsters big enough to swallow a whole ship."

"Bessie!" I laughed. "How can you believe such nonsense? You see Master Taylor with your own eyes. He's been to the New World and back again. He wasn't swallowed up by any monster."

"He was lucky."

"And I'll be even luckier! Listen, do you know what's to be found in the New World?"

"Savages," she gasped.

"Gold! Pearls! I'll scoop them up with my own hands," I said gleefully, "white pearls as large as peas. I'll keep them for you until you come. Then, then you'll be a fine lady. Bessie—think of it—you'll dress in velvet and silk." I reached for her small, moist hand. "People will call you Lady Elizabeth. We'll live together in a fine house. . . ."

"And may I have a coach," she asked, "with four horses?"

I wondered whether there were any horses in the New World, and I recognized the full extent of my ignorance, and with it a strange, creeping fear.

"I suppose so," I replied, keeping my voice light. "So now," I said with authority, "you must learn to cook and sew and tend the garden. You must be ready to do all those things so you can keep house for us. Will you be ready? Will you come?"

"Oh, yes, William," she breathed. "And please, will you write me a letter?"

"I will," I promised. "Ships will return to England for supplies, and I'll send you a letter, maybe even a token from the New World. Now go to bed, Bessie."

She walked toward me slowly, purposefully. Then, with a quick gesture, she grasped the chain she always wore around her neck and pulled it over her head.

She held it out to me. The cross, of finely wrought silver, gleamed in the firelight. "Take this," she said firmly, "and wear it always until I come to you."

"Bessie!" I hesitated, knowing that she had never been without it since the day our mother died.

Father had slipped it around Bessie's neck, murmuring, "God be with you, poor child."

Now Bessie slipped it over my head and whispered, "God be with you, William."

My throat tightened, and I wanted to hold her close. But quickly she turned to go, holding herself tall and proud. Her effort to appear womanly made her seem even more childlike. From the doorway she said, "Oh, William, you are so brave!"

I sat alone, staring into the fire. Brave? The word made me smile. No, no it wasn't courage at all that made me want to go adventuring. Far from it! The very thought of coming face to face with a savage made my mouth go dry. But to escape people like Svenson and the constable——to strike out on my own and build a name for myself—to gather the gold and pearls that would make me a gentleman! These desires were even stronger than my fear.

"Vanity is a sin, my child, and virtue its own reward." The memory of my mother's words came with the rustling of the fire.

"All the wealth of this world is as nothing before the Lord."

Mother! I have to go. Would you say that I must stay here and face the sheriff? Would you call me cowardly and irresponsible? I *will* be responsible. I'll work hard. I'll send for Bessie and take care of her. I promise you.

* * *

The next day I went to a seaman's shop and outfitted myself for the voyage. Two shirts, a pair of sturdy breeches, a cap, a knife and the most essential tools took nearly all the coins in my pouch. At Bessie's insistence, we went to the stalls and bought three bundles of seeds.

"You must begin a garden at once," Bessie told me earnestly. "I want it ready when I come."

I agreed. It would be a link between us, something real waiting for her. I, too, could imagine my little garden growing, waiting for Bessie to come and tend it.

With my last few pennies I bought bright ribbons for her hair and a pair of gloves like those worn by ladies of fashion. They really were women's gloves and much too large for Bessie. But she was determined to have them. "I shall not wear them until my voyage," she said firmly. "I'll put them away. And when my hands have grown to fit them, then . . . then. . . ."

When we came to the meeting place on that morning of departure, my spirits were very low. I suppose I had expected a grand farewell. I had envisioned heroic banners waving, and maybe a trumpet call.

But the horses were stamping, drivers were cursing, and drunken idlers emerged from the taverns to poke at each other while they leered at us. And we were a wretched-looking group. Our wagons were patched and creaking, our animals bony and wild eyed. On the faces of the colonists I saw again and again the same expression: a haunted, hungry look with tight-lipped mouths and darting, suspicious eyes. Apparently Raleigh's men had combed the countryside to enlist beggars and poor yeomen farmers as settlers. All my sense of triumph at being one of the company was drained away.

I was given a place in one of the coaches. Then came the moment of farewell. Bessie did not cry. She stood among the others, waving and smiling. The coach began to roll and sway, and I peered back at Bessie as her figure diminished. I saw the flash of the red ribbon in her hair. Then the coach rounded a corner, and I could see only the dust rising behind us.

FOUR

HUGH AND CLEMENT rode with John Brooke, the shoemaker. Brooke, with a black woolen cap perched on the back of his head, had the look of a man who had seen everything and was proud to be himself. Dressed always in his cap and smock, he had a way of standing back on his heels, observing everyone half in amusement.

Brooke and several others had been to Virginia with Master Taylor the year before. Thus, Hugh and Clement had a good start at forming friendships.

As for me—I told myself I was glad that John Brooke's coach was full. I would make it on my own from the start, and not rely on Hugh and Clement. But I soon found it is a hard thing to be among strangers. People took me into their coach, but grudgingly. My presence stole space, made them more uncomfortable.

One of the men attempted at least a civil remark. "So, you're off to the New World, are you? And what might your name be?" But that was the end of it, and I sat with my eyes straight ahead, braced against the swaying of the coach.

As we traveled south, our caravan grew, and the more people we had join us, the more alone I felt. Many knew each other, or at least had something in common. Yeomen farmers immediately found each other. The women, too, huddled together, peering about with hard, suspicious eyes. And no wonder. From snatches of conversation I knew they had reason enough to be cautious.

Among the colonists were two thieves, recruited from Colchester Prison. Three others, by their swagger, were obviously gamblers. And God only knew how many others were roustabouts, drunkards, beggars and scoundrels!

When we stopped to rest the horses at midday and I saw the assembled company, my despair was even greater than at the time of parting. Among all the men—nearly a hundred of them—were only sixteen women. I thought if our future were as dreary as the faces of those women, God help us!

They were dressed, all but three, in drab homespun, all carrying bundles, two clutching at wriggling little boys, one holding an infant. From Hugh and Clement I learned their names.

Jane Jones, the doctor's wife, had a habit of repeating whatever anyone said. Her mouth turned down and her eyes rolled heavenward, and she looked as strong as any peasant woman.

"Ah, what a dear little mite!" she exclaimed to Joyce Archard beside her. "May I see him? May I hold him? He's a large babe, and you must be weary."

But Mistress Archard, another gray wren of a woman, firmly shook her head. "No, thank you, but he wants his Mum."

"Wants his Mum, does he?" Mistress Jones tugged at her white kerchief. "Wants his Mum."

"He's not eating proper," continued Mistress Archard, and the frown line between her heavy brows deepened.

"Not eating," repeated Mistress Jones, and as if on signal, the baby began to cry in loud, strong wails. Mistress Archard began to shake and bounce it so hard that I thought the baby would drop out of its swaddling. Instead, it grew quiet immediately, and Mistress Archard looked up to catch me watching her.

I nodded slightly, and she looked down again, seeming distressed and embarrassed. Several times when we stopped to rest, I saw her looking at me. Then always she'd turn away quickly again, shifting the baby, shaking him, insisting to all the women in turn, "No, thank you, but he wants his Mum."

After the first, our days of travel seemed so long that any change at all was welcome. One of the wagons lost a wheel; the wagon behind plowed into it, causing a terrible uproar. Everyone gathered to shout out advice and to complain about the delay.

Only the owner of the wagon, George Howe, seemed composed and even good natured as he set about making repairs.

John Brooke, rocking back on his heels, watched the scene with a smile. Beside him stood Hugh, calling out, "Steady there, mind those horses!" but his advice was lost in the general roar.

"Fine fellow," Hugh said, jerking his thumb toward George Howe, the young, lanky fellow clad in a leather cloak. "He's an Assistant, you know. Always beaming, positively beaming with good humor."

"He's got a lot to be jolly about, I guess," I said, thinking that for one so young to be an Assistant was an enviable beginning.

"That just proves you shouldn't judge too quickly," put in the shoemaker. "See that boy?" He nodded toward a lad of about eleven, whose left foot was crippled. "That's George Howe's son, Georgie. The mother was killed in a fire. And the boy . . ." Brooke tapped his head. "He's a bit—you know."

"Stutters," Hugh added. "But the father's very nice. You'll see. He goes out of his way to meet everyone. He's already asked me about you."

"Has he?" The thought that anyone should care to ask about me lifted my spirits, but I soon fell back to feeling half sick from the dust, the stink of horses, the rumbling and swaying. I would be glad never to ride in a coach again.

At one rest stop I was nearly left behind. In getting out, some careless brute had slammed the coach door on my finger. First I felt nothing, then there were searing flashes of pain, and in moments my finger began to swell and turn blue. Hugh and Clement were nowhere to be seen; probably drinking at the tavern, I thought, outraged from pain. I stumbled toward Dr. Jones, who barely glanced at my finger and said, "It will mend."

"It will mend," repeated his wife. Glaring, blowing on my poor finger, I left them.

"Mud's a good remedy," came a voice, and lanky George Howe walked toward me, followed by his son, and by a tan-colored dog of middle size.

The dog began to sniff me thoroughly, and George Howe laughed. "He's chosen you for a friend! Come on, Lap, over here, that's a boy," he said as the dog leaped into his arms and began to lick his face.

"Where will I find mud?" I asked.

The boy pointed a finger. "Th-th-*there!*"

"Quite right, Georgie," said the father, beaming. "Just behind us a bit is a small stream." He examined my finger closely. "Yes, go and bathe it in the mud. We'll come with you if you want company," he said smiling, and immediately I felt I'd like nothing better than to spend some time with him.

But the boy began to tug at his father's arm and whispered something in his ear. "Of course, Georgie, come along then," said the father. "I'm sorry," he told me, smiling again. "You just go along. We'll have plenty of time to talk later."

The mud pack did ease the ache, and it was good

to sit quietly beside the stream, away from the noise and the dust. Perhaps I almost wanted to be left behind. At any rate, next thing I saw the cloud of dust that meant they had started, and I leaped to my feet, running behind the last coach, shouting, "Wait for me! Wait, blast you, wait!"

At last the coach creaked to a halt only long enough for me to climb inside. With a violent forward lurch it continued, and I jolted backward to find myself facing Elinor Dare. Beside her sat Agnes Wood, and opposite, Mistress Archard with the baby.

Elinor Dare nodded, bade me good day.

I took off my cap, and she at once noticed my discolored finger. "Emme Merrimoth will have something for you to put on that," she said.

"Is she an apothecary?" I asked.

"Oh, I hardly think so," Elinor said. "But she has a satchel full of bottles and powders."

I had seen the old crone with her huge tapestry bag. Her upper arms were thick as a man's thigh, flabby and loose. Wild graying hair stood out in all directions, and her well-padded shape was further padded by countless petticoats.

"Thank you," I said. "I'll go to her at the next stop."

But Agnes Wood began to mutter in her wailing singsong. "A heathen woman, I've seen the likes of her before. A witch, with her powders and potions—take care. . . ."

Elinor Dare slapped her hands together, flashing

a fierce look at the servant. "Nonsense!" she cried. "What nonsense and slander!"

The conversation seemed to terrify Mistress Archard. The crease between her brows deepened, and as she stiffened the baby began to scream.

"Now see what you've done," said Elinor, though softly.

In return, through the screaming of the baby, Agnes Wood wailed again, "I've pledged my life to your father's service, but who's to save her when the time is near? Who? Who?"

The coach hit a rut, swayed crazily from side to side. The baby's head banged hard against the pane, making it redouble its screams. This was madness! I was caught in this stifling contraption with three mad women and a howling child, doomed to this horrible chorus of wailing and screaming. God, why would any man in his right mind want to take women on a voyage! My finger throbbed, my head ached.

"Stop!"

Suddenly everything was quiet.

"William, make him stop the coach," said Mistress Dare, pale and trembling.

I banged on the panel. The coach reeled once, then stopped dead, and Elinor Dare fled to a large tree by the roadside. I saw her shoulders heaving as she retched.

* * *

What I wouldn't have given to tell Bessie! Somehow her parting gift stirred a great deal of interest. I suppose it labeled me in a way. People knew nothing about me; I was "the boy—the one with the silver cross."

It was the cross that caught Jane Pierce's eye as we arrived at last at Portsmouth. Hugh had told me the gossip. The dark-haired, flashing-eyed widow Pierce was rumored to be the sister of our captain, Ferdinando. She wore many rings on her fingers, and was always surrounded by groups of men. They laughed heartily at her rapid speech and her fluttering hands.

"She owned a curio shop in London," Hugh told me, "though she's a Spaniard, like the Captain." A sarcastic note came into Hugh's voice at the word "Spaniard."

Several large trunks belonged to the widow Pierce, filled with items of her trade. She seemed to be engaging in a lively trade even as we traveled. Whenever we stopped she'd run into one of the shops, coming out with a smile and a parcel.

From the moment of our arrival in Portsmouth, everything was total confusion. Assistants rushed about looking busy and important, checking off lists, answering every question with, "You'll have to see the Governor about that." Travelers scurried after their possessions, begging the sailors to be careful in loading. Some went to trade their horses. Others suddenly remembered necessities and rushed to the dockside shops and stalls.

I stood outside the shops whose wares overflowed onto low benches and tables, struck with the awful feeling that this was my last chance. I needed and wanted everything, but my pockets were empty. And the merchants hawked and coaxed, "How about this fine woolen cap? You'll not find one like it where you're going!"

I was sure of that. When again would I ever see such a splendid array of goods? How easy it would be, I thought in a flash, to pick a pocket, just this once, and immediately I felt my face burning with shame.

"William! William Wythers!"

The patter of feet followed the shrill voice, and the widow Pierce caught my arm. "William," she said in her rapid way, "would you be so good as to enter that shop over there and inquire about the price of the blue porcelain locket? Yes, the large one in the shape of a circle." She looked me up and down, then said gaily, "I would judge you as a good actor."

"Actor?" I echoed.

"You might say 'tis for your sweetheart, and of course, you haven't much money. But oh, you must have a token to leave with her, for your heart is breaking with love, and you've nothing to give her before you set out on your long voyage!"

Her dark eyes grew even larger, and she looked so droll in her imitation of a heartsick lover that I laughed and said, "Very well. I'll do it."

Quickly she pressed several coins into my hand and whispered, "I'll reward you, William! I must have that locket."

I rather enjoyed my role, and emerged victorious,

the locket in my hand and several coins left over. "Splendid!" she cried, her face beaming. "Ah, you're a clever one, and here's a shilling for you."

Then, thoughtfully, she gazed at the cross around my neck, held out her hand as if to touch it, and I had the feeling that the cross was what had interested her all along. "If the time comes," she said, "when you want to part with that token, I'll do well for you."

"Thank you," I said, fingering the cross, "but I will keep it always."

"Always?" She smiled. "Always is a long, long time." She turned, seeming to glide, holding her swaying skirts as she went to tell her friends of her newest treasure.

I pondered for over an hour about how to spend my shilling, and deliberated whether to buy several small things or one large one. But the dockside shops were very expensive. At last I bought a tin cup for my shilling—the last thing I was ever to buy for money.

* * *

We stood on the dock, watching the boat pitch up and down in the water. Its keel rose and sank, and for a moment I felt my mouth go sour. It seemed that the ship was lying calm, but that the planks under my feet and the sky beyond were tilting crazily from side to side.

Suddenly I heard a crash, followed by a cry. Then the women, who had been clustered together like a covey of wrens, broke away and rushed toward the gangway where somebody's household goods lay smashed and scattered.

I moved with the others. The next moment I felt something warm and heavy thrust into my arms, and I heard Mistress Archard's fretful voice telling me, "You! You take him!"

She ran off, and I was left in a near panic with the damp-bottomed baby, thinking, what if she doesn't come back?

But she had only run toward the pile of possessions, where she knelt down over the broken plates and crockery. At last her husband, Arnold Archard, was beside her murmuring clumsily, "Joyce, ah, Joyce, what a terrible pity. Your precious cups, ah well, a-well."

She didn't speak; she didn't cry. But her face hardened and she seemed even to have forgotten about the child. It stirred in my arms, let out a single cry, and immediately I tossed it as I'd seen its mother do.

From the fringe of spectators Emme Merrimoth called in her loud, breezy voice, "It's good luck then! Good luck to our voyage, and thanks to Mistress Archard for supplying it!"

I became aware of a strange sickening odor as, more gently now, I rocked the baby. Then I saw its source. Around the baby's neck hung an amulet, a filthy bundle of herbs and animal hair.

She was back, took the baby and said softly, "Thank you, William Wythers."

Why had she chosen me? Hugh strode up,

laughing at my dismay. He clapped me on the back and shouted, "So, you've become a nursemaid, Willie!"

His voice was too loud, his swagger too self-important. And he'd never in his life called me Willie!

I turned, ready with a sharp retort. Then I saw the reason for his playacting. Watching us with a frankly appraising smile was Margaret Lawrence.

To this day I cannot properly describe Margaret Lawrence. Oh, I can say that her hair was pale, the color of corn silk, that her eyes were moody. Were they gray? Blue? Green? All of these—they changed from day to day, from moment to moment. She was a changeling. Shy and distant one moment, furious or demanding the next, she always remained unreachable and captivating. Every man wanted her. And she knew full well her power.

I stood a little taller, made a joke to Hugh, felt myself bold, daring, good looking—William Wythers, carpenter, adventurer, *pirate!* Then I became aware of the tin cup I still held in my hand, saw Margaret Lawrence turn away to join Christopher Cooper, the pompous young gentleman from Oxford who rode a marvelous horse. There was a taste of dust and metal in my mouth. And then they called on us to board: first the Assistants and the gentlemen, lawyers, doctor, tradesmen, farmers. At last I heard my name shouted out along the docks.

"William Wythers! Pauper!"

FIVE

WILLIAM WYTHERS, *pauper!* My dreams of making a new beginning vanished in that word, and my humiliation was increased when someone shouted roughly, "Boy! Give a hand here, be quick!"

I struggled with a heavy barrel, consoling myself that at least I hadn't been assigned to the pinnace, the smallest of our three ships, which would surely toss and swirl like a cork at sea. I was to travel on our flagship, *The Lion*, with Hugh. Clement had been assigned to the flyboat. I couldn't imagine why the brothers had to be separated. Was it simply because our high-handed Assistants and "gentlemen" delighted in being mean!

Angry at everyone, I gave the barrel a violent shove.

"You there!" came another order. "Look lively, help him with that thing."

Slowly, sullenly, Tom Smart pushed aside his wild heap of thatch-colored hair. He was about fourteen, and I'd never seen him without that smirk on his face. In a clear, bold tone he called back, "I'm not obliged to work for my passage. My father has paid it!"

He surely had a big mouth for a skinny half-pint of a fellow, traveling alone without protection. I looked around, expecting someone to brain him for that remark.

But next the Governor himself strode forward, frowning, pointing at the barrels. "Where's the rest of the salt, Ananais?" The man beside him hung back, as if trying to decide what to say.

"Is this all?" the Governor persisted. "I thought we had decided exactly. . . ."

"I was told we'd pick up more salt on the way," replied Ananais Dare. A few minutes earlier I'd seen him engrossed in his work and confident. A good sort, I'd thought, seeing how he listened patiently to every request. Now his sureness seemed to have melted away. Beside the robust Governor, he looked too lean. Only his hands and muscle-knotted arms confirmed his trade; he was a tiler and bricklayer.

"Who told you we'd take on salt along the way?" asked the Governor. His tone had become milder, but with effort.

"The Captain," replied Ananais, facing his father-in-law fully for the first time. "He said we'd take more salt in the Indies. He knows a place."

The Governor's lips tightened, then he said wearily, "Very well, Ananais." He put his hand on his son-in-law's back, as if to make it up to him, but I saw Ananais stiffen.

"Carry on, then," the Governor shouted, and he motioned for several men to help me. "Come on—can't you see this is too heavy for him?" He paused to tell my name and occupation to Ananais, who thrust out his hand and said, "We'll need your craft, William, when we land."

Something in the way Ananais Dare spoke to me eased my anger and humiliation. He would never call me "boy." I said a few words in greeting. He listened to me closely as he did to everyone. And I was grateful.

That gratitude, later, made me stand up for Dare when Hugh and Brooke began to criticize. "It's not the first time," said Brooke, "that I've heard of Master Dare misplacing his trust. The Gov'nor had a right to be angry. Dare should have followed orders."

I spoke up to defend him. "But if the Captain says he'll find salt along the way . . . hasn't he sailed to the New World before?"

"Aye, he has," nodded Brooke, "and he's said to know all the ports. . . ."

"But he's a Spaniard," Hugh broke in. Again he gave the word "Spaniard" an ugly twist, and several men who'd gathered around agreed that Ananais Dare should not have depended on a Spaniard even though he was Captain of our fleet.

"Of course, Dare is an Assistant," said John Brooke, "and he's got the right to make decisions."

"Decisions!" cried Maurice Allen, a small, dark-bearded man who also had been to Virginia the year before. "That one makes no decisions without his father-in-law." He laughed. "Well, I'd give up my independence, too, for a comely young wife like Mistress Elinor."

The men laughed and winked at each other, and Maurice Allen passed around seeds and nuts from the bag he always carried. His teeth were quite black from them, and bits of shell stuck in between them.

Always, the talk turned to Spaniards, to King Philip and our Queen. Feeling ignorant, I only listened. Some of the men never said the word "Spanish" without adding "dog." And at the sound someone else would always spit. They talked about a great sea battle at Cádiz that I knew nothing about, though even Hugh seemed to know it all.

"What I wouldn't have given to be with Drake at Cádiz!" he sighed, caressing his sword. "They sailed right into the harbor and took Philip's fleet by surprise."

Finger uplifted, Maurice Allen put in, "But only a small part of Philip's fleet was taken at Cádiz."

"But it serves as a lesson, gentlemen!" cried the Assistant Christopher Cooper. "King Philip talks about building an invincible armada. Invincible! Bah."

Richard Berry, our muster captain—the one who had labeled me "pauper"—stood up stiff as a ramrod and said, "We could find ourselves in a very difficult position. King Philip needs his store of gold and silver from the New World. He won't take kindly to the thought of English colonies."

"Let him choke on us then!" said his brother, Henry, pudgy faced and high spirited. "I'll bet our fleet against Philip's any day."

"You may have to do more than that," said his brother sternly, but Henry only laughed.

"All this is behind us," he said happily. "We're off to the New World, don't you know?"

* * *

On shipboard there's no such thing as privacy, no such thing as silence. Everything creaks and groans and shifts, and the water slaps endlessly against the hull, even when it is calm. At night, too, come the restless sounds of people stirring in their sleep, groaning, dreaming, coughing. You can't move without bumping someone's leg or an arm. The slightest whisper seems to echo in the hot, tight quarters, and then comes the irritated chorus of grumbling sleepers, "Quiet down! Shut up there, can't you let us sleep?"

Incredibly, the others were quite soon able to settle down on their bundles or mats of straw. For me, sleep was impossible. I had found myself a corner by the bosun's storeroom, but my legs were cramped, and the low timbers overhead made it a sweltering box. Near me, Hugh had found himself a low shelf, and he slept there. Only a few had cabins—the wealthy men like John Spendlove; the Governor, of course; and the Assistants. But the walls were thin, and we soon learned that anything revealed inside one of those cabins quickly became public knowledge. John Sampson, the carpenter, for example, happened to have a boil on his back. Before he knew it, Emme Merrimoth ran to him with her herbs, and the shoemaker offered to lance it for him.

As I lay sleeping one night, I became aware of a faint weeping. A voice rumbled, another replied. Words were lost among the creaking of the ship, until sharply I heard Elinor Dare's familiar voice crying, "But Ananais, I only did it for you, so that we could be together!"

"But you deceived me!" came the loud answer. "If I'd known, I would never have let you. . . ."

The ship heaved; something rolled across the deck with a clatter, the restless sleepers stirred. Bits of straw prickled through my clothing. I slapped at the army of small biting insects. At last I stood up, and unaccustomed to the low timbers, banged my head on them. Cursing, I stumbled out, and Hugh grunted, "Who's that?"

Instantly he swung himself upright, hand on his sword, and I grinned to myself at his readiness, even here, to defend himself.

"It's only me," I whispered. "I'm going on deck."

"I'll go with you," he said. "Can't sleep in this hole."

"You? You've been snoring away."

"Come on. Let's get some air."

We stood at the rail for a long time, watching the

stars. I had never seen so many of them, or the sky so black. I breathed deeply of the fresh, cool air.

Where am I? What am I doing here? I asked myself. I felt as if part of me were someplace else, or asleep.

"Hugh," I said.

"Yes."

Maybe he felt the same as I. Without someone familiar nearby, a person could lose himself. It was good to have him beside me, just standing there without speaking. Here, in the vast darkness, we didn't dare talk about where we were going. It was all so strange.

We talked, instead, about silly, unimportant things. Then Hugh said, grinning, "You know, William, you and I should have gotten ourselves wives before we came. Winter nights in Virginia are very cold, I hear."

I nodded dumbly, embarrassed at my lack of experience with women.

"Of course," he continued, "more women will come with the next group of recruits. And I suppose, meanwhile, some of our men will bed down with savage wenches. You should hear the tales they tell about last year! I do wonder," he mused, "how much of it was true. I mean—can you imagine getting near a *savage?*"

I swallowed, hard. "No." He expected more, and I said, "I mean, a savage is—is not like—like other people."

"Of course not."

"But yet they are human." It was half-question, half-statement.

"I've heard two different opinions on the matter," Hugh said. "My father says they are definitely human, though, of course, not fully formed."

I pondered this for a long time, and at last I wondered aloud, "But, if they are really human, why are they so different from us?"

"We'll soon find out for ourselves, William, won't we?" he said, moving his sword to make it flash in the moonlight.

* * *

We sailed to the Isle of Wight, then to Plymouth, always taking on more supplies. On May 8 we headed out to the open sea. If we were lucky, we would see Virginia in two months' time.

The close life of shipboard was hard on Hugh. He paced endlessly on the deck, searching for the open spaces that didn't exist. And he wanted his brother, though he would never admit it. "I wonder what old Clement's doing?" he'd say. "Maybe he's taken over the galley; maybe he's baking bread for the crew. Maybe it's better on the flyboat. I hear Captain Spicer's a good man."

But how could it be better? Life at sea is miserable. How often during those days I thanked God that I had decided not to be a sailor. There is a viciousness on shipboard that comes out soon after you're under way. The lap and the smell of the water become sickening; soon food tastes like paste with salt. The sun can be unmercifully hot, sweat soaks your clothing, plasters your hair, drips from your face. Then the wind comes up, whipping away your very thoughts, hurling objects across the deck. On calm days you feel as if you're floating inside a great bowl. And everything becomes hateful. Men fight at nothing.

One chews his nails. The sight becomes unbearable, and a fight is on. I saw men beat each other bloody over an extra helping of pudding. Let one man hang his cloak on a clothes hook put up by another, and the owner of that hook will knock him senseless. And with women aboard—well. . . .

I was stuck midway between the boys and the men; too old for children's games, too young to be counted. But every sailor knew my name.

"Wythers! Steady on those kegs!"

"Wythers! Hang on the line there."

"Wythers! There's caulking to do."

The smell of tar and pitch ground into my clothing. The horses on deck caused unbelievable filth, and someone had to shovel up after. When the seams had been caulked, the deck had to be scrubbed and rust scoured away. There were ropes to mend, ropes to fetch, ropes to coil. And when all was done we started again. Meanwhile, there was always oakum to pick to keep a good supply of the loose rope fibers ready for caulking the seams. So my daily life went around in a circle. It seemed to me that the whole ship depended for its survival on two things; the first was rope; the second, myself, William Wythers.

In that dreadful sameness day after day, one begins to look forward to the strangest things. The supper bell arouses great joy. The sight of a leaping fish, or just a green swirl on the water, brings the excitement of a bear baiting. I even welcomed the mischief of the three little boys on board.

Bobby Ellis, the youngest, was about seven. He always wore a fresh white collar, though his mother was dead and he'd come with his father. He'd hang back, undecided, then go along with the other two; but he never really enjoyed the pranks, for he'd been taught to be good. Tom Humphrey, who also had only a father, was a loose-limbed fellow. Easy going, he seemed to flap rather than walk. He was game for anything. But the one I liked best was Ambrose Viccars. And he was the worst rascal of the lot.

Ambrose would sit quietly on a keg wearing an old sailor's cap much too big for him. Freckle faced, beaming from deep inside, he'd be working out a plot. Soon there'd be a dead rat in someone's bedding, or a cask undone, or a game of catch that involved lemons stolen from the galley.

Twice I had to haul Ambrose down from the rigging, while below his mother stood threatening, then pleading. Both times he came down at last, after she'd promised not to whip him. But then his father did.

The three boys followed me around. "We've come to help you, William!"

"Then shovel it up," I'd shout, "and stop stamping it all over the deck!"

"We'll scrub with you, William!"

"Look out! For God's sake, we've just finished that part! Ambrose, you're soaked. Why did you make Bobby drink that awful water?"

One day I gave them each a brush and a bucket of water. "All right," I said sternly. "You want to help. So paint the deck, go on. Hurry! This is special paint, keeps it from rusting."

It was two or three hours before they caught on. That night my young friends brought me a special bit of duff, nicely seasoned with currants. I'd eaten half before I took off after Ambrose, roaring, threatening to hang him upside down from the mast. Those currants I'd eaten turned out to be dead flies.

One afternoon, as I was putting away the buckets in the storeroom, I heard a faint scratching. Ambrose, I thought, or maybe rats. Rats gnawed at the ropes, fouled our grain, frightened the horses and made the women shriek. The scratching did not seem to be important. It had been one of those windy days when everything rolls from port to starboard, and the clattering can drive you mad. But now the sea was calm again, and I looked forward to sitting alone on deck and carving. In late afternoon, Margaret Lawrence always took a stroll on the deck. True, she was never alone, but a few days before she had stopped to look at my carving. And she had nodded and smiled.

I put up the buckets, thinking only of that smile, and I heard a sneeze.

"Who's there? Ambrose," I roared, "come out of

there or I'll haul you out, and this time I'll whip you proper!"

I heard nothing, then a sniff. Silently I lifted myself onto one of the kegs and looked down, but I couldn't see anything.

I reached down into the darkness, felt something warm and wriggling, grasped for it, and suddenly I was bitten on the hand. Hot for vengeance now, I hung over nearly to the floorboards, grasped a handful of hair and began to pull.

"Stop! Ow! Ow! Leave go!"

There followed a string of curses that even Ambrose wouldn't know, and sure enough, it wasn't his voice or his shape, but a taller person, a stranger.

"Come out!" I panted, and as he lifted himself up over the keg I took him by the collar and pulled him over, hard. He sank down, shivering, a dirty bundle of rags and matted hair, eyes deep and hollow.

I thought to grasp him by the collar and pay him back for that bite, then decided just to go above and leave him there. Why couldn't I just have a few minutes of peace at the end of a long day? To be found with a stowaway would only mean trouble. Who would believe I hadn't been involved? Governor White had said my past would be forgotten, but I knew better. So far I'd kept out of trouble, but why should I let myself be marked, now, at the beginning of this venture?

I turned, walked along the dark, heaving passage. This was no business of mine. Let someone else find the stowaway and claim the credit—or the blame.

Surely the sailors would find him. What an idiot he was, to think he could hide away for months aboard a ship. The sailors would find him, and then. . . .

Sunday last we'd witnessed the punishment of two sailors caught shirking. That night I hadn't slept at all; the whole affair at Rochester kept going through my head.

From the end of the passage I turned to look back. He was still sitting there, head down on his hands, listing to one side. A strange feeling came over me, a giddiness. Slowly I turned back until I stood over him. "What's your name?" I asked gruffly. "Where did you come on board? How did you think to hide away like this?" I fought back the temptation to slap him, and I couldn't understand my own anger.

He said nothing. Rather, both hands rose up to his face, pulled back at his hair from the center. Something about the shape of those hands, and especially that gesture, made me gasp. I'd seen Bessie using her hands that way, parting her hair from the center to pull it back over her shoulders. Even if her hair had been cropped, it would take months to lose that habit.

My voice now came in a whispering croak. "You're—a girl."

Again, no reply, but the thin arms were hugged tight around the chest, and I knew I was right. Not that she was womanly! Thin as a rail and flat chested, no curve to her hips, but still there were those arched brows and long lashes and slim hands.

I only heard a deep, wavering sigh, and for an instant she looked up at me. What to do? Leave her, leave her for someone else to discover, I decided. One of the little boys might find her, or one of the sailors. And if the sailors found her. . . .

Well, she was clearly a vagabond, probably a harlot . . . and then I thought of Bessie, how she looked when she cried, how she hated to be alone. But why me? This isn't Bessie! She was crying silently, tears and more tears, but no sound. I never could bear to hear crying, or to see it!

"Come on," I said at last. "I suppose I can take you to . . ."

But the decision was out of my hands, for in that moment I heard the rude stamping of feet, the swaggering voices of two of the sailors, and suddenly they were upon us.

SIX

THEY WERE GLEEFUL at the discovery, at the excitement promised by a stowaway. They hauled her up by the neck, pinned her arms behind her, and while one held her the other stepped back, fist poised.

"No!" I screamed out. "It's a girl!"

The change that swept over the sailor's face was astounding. His flabby face, stupid as a bull's, took on a sheen of excitement.

We were dragged up the ladder. That bull of a sailor held my arms behind me, dragged me backward, so that my head banged against the slats.

We were pulled past the sailors on duty, their faces grim and set. Past several men of our company, bent over a game of chance—they glanced up only briefly, uncaring.

But Ambrose Viccars caught sight of us, lunged at the sailor who held me, flew at him with his fists, screaming at the top of his lungs, "Let him go, you dirty big ox! Let him go, you stinking son of a. . . ."

One kick from the sailor's boot sent Ambrose flying. The movement threw me, sprawling, on the deck, and this angered the sailor even more. He lifted his boot. I saw the thick black underside, turned my face down to the deck.

A voice, calm and cool, but filled with a strange power halted everything. "If I were you, friend," the voice intoned, "I'd leave him be."

It was George Howe, chewing a straw, his long gangling legs spread wide against the swaying of the ship. Something in his attitude made the sailor drop back and say gruffly, "We're just takin' him and a stowaway to the Captain's quarters."

George said nothing more. But he walked behind us, still chewing that straw, until the sailor's knock was answered with a loud "Come!" and I found myself inside the Captain's cabin.

I had seen the Captain before, of course, at the bridge or standing on the deck. Whenever talk turned to "Spanish dogs," and the other men scoffed at our Captain, Ananais Dare would say, "He runs a good ship, and that's all that need concern us."

It was true. At the Captain's approach, the sailors on watch rose a little taller, those at the rigging strained their muscles and bent their backs. Captain Ferdinando's usual pose was one of gazing far over the horizon. A question by one of the mates would startle him back to the present. He would listen, then laugh.

His laughter could be heard along the deck in many varieties. I thought I'd never seen a more jovial man. From deep in his belly he'd laugh, then throw back his head and flail his arms with laughter. At other times the laughter was held inside, escaping in little bursts, and his dark eyes would be brimming with it.

Now his head was bent over his charts, and slowly he scanned them, tracing the lines with his ringed index finger. I felt no fear, only impatience. I'd explain the whole thing easily, and that brute of a sailor would be punished for the way he'd treated me. I'd seen Captain Ferdinando bow courteously before the ladies. And whenever a traveler had a request, the Captain would listen, bow stiffly and say, "Yes, I'll certainly attend to it. Be assured, it will be done."

At last the Captain looked up, and the sailors explained their mission. The Captain's eyes were focused at a distance. But at the word "stowaway," and then "female" he shot up out of his chair and began, peculiarly, to laugh. Small fits of laughter seethed inside of him, burst out from between his lips, shook his frame from the inside like a fever. I suddenly felt a stab of horror. From somewhere in my past I recalled the words, "Beware of a man who laughs too much!"

"A stowaway! A female!" His moustache twitched, then his eyes flashed onto me for a moment. He moved toward the girl with the swiftness of a bat, swooped down, and in one motion lifted her chin and slapped her across the face.

She reeled back, but did not cry out. Her lips were puffed and swollen.

Now in the silence I heard the boards creak. I heard the harsh breath of the sailors through their open mouths. The Captain backed away around his desk, flung himself into the chair, and gazed into the distance. Still the boards creaked. Water in a basin slapped to and fro. Then he spoke in hardly more than a whisper.

"You know what's done with stowaways and such." The soft, smooth voice flowed, filled the cabin. "Take her below—you know the place. She will be put off at Santa Cruz. As for him. . . ."

Laughter again threatened at the edges of his lips, and my head was ringing, *speak out, he means you! Be silent! Beware of a man who laughs too much.*

"Captain!" I cried out. "I only found her as I was going about my work."

In that moment the door burst open, and Governor White stood there. "Captain, I must talk with you. There's no sign of our flyboat. I've asked one of the mates, and it seems we've lost her. She hasn't been sighted since the Bay of Portugal."

The Captain smiled. " 'Twas foggy in the Bay," he said.

"Captain, you may understand that I'm very concerned about my colonists on that ship."

"Never mind," said Ferdinando, laughing. "Never mind."

"Do you mean, sir, that they're taking another

course? But we are the flagship . . . have you sighted them, Captain?"

Captain Ferdinando raised his head high, looked above the Governor's head to a spot on the wall. "My duty, Governor, is to take these planters to Virginia. Captain Spicer knows how to sail a ship. Let him take the wind, then, and follow our lead."

"Captain Spicer has never been to Virginia before!" the Governor objected. "And I'm responsible for the safety of my colonists on that ship!"

"No," replied the Captain, facing the Governor squarely. "Your command begins only after we reach Virginia. I am responsible for proceeding in all haste, for landing the planters and returning my crew to England before winter. It is my duty."

"Captain, I implore you, if only we could lay at anchor for a day or so. . . ."

Laughter exploded, and even the sailors smiled. "In this wind?" cried Ferdinando. "Oh, protect us from painters who would be sea captains! We'll put in at Santa Cruz," he concluded, "as swiftly as possible." He turned now to me and the girl. "As you can see, Governor, we have a stowaway, another harlot. She'll be put off at Santa Cruz."

"No! I'm not what you say!" The girl began to cry, twisting her hands. "I want to go to the New World! I'll work for you. I can cook and carry water and wash clothes. I'm *strong*."

"Captain, can't we discuss this girl at another time?" The Governor's eyes swept helplessly over the cabin. "My colonists. . . ."

"I'll attend to them, Governor. Be assured . . . now, if you will kindly clear my cabin, I've work to do. You may wish to consider whether you will pay passage for this—this stowaway, or else. . . . My second mate will come to you in half an hour for your answer."

The Governor led me and the girl to his cabin, where he paced wordlessly for several minutes. Then he went to his cupboard, took forth a plate of hard biscuits and said to the girl, "Eat."

I watched her tear at the food like a ravenous dog. And then Governor White questioned her.

"Tell me your name," he said.

"Elizabeth Glane."

"Your father?"

She paused. "I don't know."

"Your mother?"

"Dead."

"Are you a pauper? Alone?"

She nodded.

"How old are you?"

Another pause. "Seventeen, sir."

"Don't lie to me," the Governor said sternly. Then his face softened. "I have a daughter of my own. I think I can still tell the difference between a woman and a girl."

"Nearly fifteen, sir," the girl admitted.

"Fourteen, then, eh?"

She nodded.

"Have you committed a crime, Elizabeth?"

"Oh, no, sir, never! I'm not—not what the Captain said."

Little by little her story came out. She had been working in a tavern at Portsmouth, and one day. . . .

"A kindly man came in, sir. He said I was to work for him. He said the tavern was an evil place, not the sort of place for a girl like me. So I went with him, thinking he wanted a servant girl, but. . . ."

He had used her in his swindling, sending her into taverns to befriend ignorant farmers or sailors on leave. He would enter then, pretending she was his niece, lost and found again. In gratitude, he'd buy the stranger a drink.

Governor White nodded and said, "It's an old game. Soon they would wager over something, a game of cards, all in good fellowship to start with."

"That's right!" Elizabeth Glane cried. "It was always the same, until . . ."

"Until he had robbed the poor simpleton of all his coins," White nodded. "The ports are infested with those swindlers. But why didn't you leave him?"

"He said I'd be accused the same as he," the girl replied. "He said nobody would believe me, and that I'd end in prison."

She had heard about our voyage and seen our ships at anchor. She had cut off her hair and gone, dressed like a boy, to be hired as a cabin boy. "They said there was no place for me," the girl continued, "so in the crowd I just came on and hid."

"Well, what am I to do with you?" the Governor demanded, sounding completely vexed. "I suppose you could work off your passage, but who's to look out for you? A girl like you—barely more than a child."

I was bone tired from the day's work. By now Margaret Lawrence would have finished her stroll—why couldn't I have a moment of peace at the end of the day? The girl was looking at me with those deep, frightened eyes, and I found myself thinking of Bessie again.

I stiffened, as if someone had called me. Governor White was pacing again, shaking his head. Don't look at *me!* I wanted to shout, I'm *nobody!* I'm only sixteen years old and . . . I heard the echo of my own voice, the rash promise, "I'll do whatever is expected of me, sir."

Well, surely it was not expected that I . . . but the Governor might take it as a personal favor. That wretched girl kept looking at me with Bessie's eyes, while something inside me warned, "Don't get mixed up in it," and something else answered, "That's right, don't get tied down. . . ."

But suddenly I blurted out, "I suppose I could look out for her until we land in Virginia."

The Governor stopped pacing. His brows shot up. "You?"

"Well, I found her, and I guess there's nobody else."

"Yes—if she'll just keep out of trouble. I could arrange for her passage. She could be of help to Mistress Dare," he mused.

"I'll work!" Elizabeth Glane cried out again. "I'll cook and wash and carry water."

"Very well, William," the Governor said, sighing with relief. "You understand your duty to this girl," he continued sternly. "You will regard her only as . . ." he cleared his throat meaningfully, "as a brother would regard a—sister."

I suppressed a smile. "Yes, sir," I said, hoping that this wretched girl would stop sniffling, and already cursing myself for a fool.

* * *

I had naturally thought she would want the company of women. But Elizabeth Glane followed me around like a puppy. Hugh thought it was a good joke; he teased me constantly about "my girl."

"Can't you teach your girl some manners?" he'd ask, when Elizabeth flung food scraps over her shoulder. "She'll fit in among the savages," he murmured, when Elizabeth scooped up a pudding with her fingers.

I carved a spoon for her from a bit of wood, but she wouldn't use it. She wanted me to put a hole in it so she could wear it around her neck.

She walked like a boy, wept like a girl, cursed like a sailor. She constantly picked lice out of her hair, squashed them dead, then saved the bodies to count and report, "Twelve just this morning—imagine, once I caught twenty-six!"

When Sunday came, she followed me to services, but she didn't even know how to pray. She knelt clumsily, and twice she toppled over against me as the ship swayed. And I prayed with all my might, "Oh, Lord, help me in future to keep my big mouth shut. Oh Gracious Lord, make me mind my own business. Please, Lord, make someone come along and take her off my hands."

Roger Prat, an Assistant, and a cooper by trade, made himself our preacher. And indeed, the part suited him. His full, dark beard quivered as he spoke in his fervent chant, "The voice of the Lord is upon the waters; the glory of God thundereth. The Lord is upon many waters."

We prayed, gazing over the water, for friends and relatives lost at sea. That Sunday nearly everyone came to prayers, beseeching God for the safety of our lost flyboat. "Lord, who took Jonah safely across the waters, even in the belly of the fish, guide our comrades in their distress, for the sake of Thy holy Name, we pray. . . ."

He had a marvelous, powerful, ringing voice. And I thought, if fervor alone could make a miracle, Roger Prat would accomplish it. It was a treat to watch him. And when, near sundown, he called for evening services, I went. Most of the travelers had had enough with the morning prayers. But I went, and Roger Prat beamed at me and put his hand on my head. He gazed at the cross around my neck and said, "I see you are a believer. It's a pity," he continued in his full voice, "that so few of our company know the Lord." And he waved his head toward the men lounging beside a cannon, laughing and wagering.

He seemed about to ask a question, but the others had already gathered, and he began to sing.

> *"Sing to the Lord,*
> *Sing prai-ai-aises!"*

I loved to hear him singing in his rich, deep voice. With his back arched and head thrown back, he raised up a mighty sound. In his dark cloak he reminded me somehow of a huge black whale arched up on its tail in the middle of the ocean, rising from the waves and singing.

And I felt ashamed. For the truth was that I hadn't come for religion. I came to break the boredom, and I came for the music.

Most of the women came and sat with their hands devoutly in their laps. I glanced at their faces. Mistress Archard, the line between her brows almost softened away—the widow Pierce, nodding warmly—Mistress Jones, repeating the refrains to her heart's content. And I thought, it must be easier for a woman to be good, and to believe. I wondered why they had been chosen not to feel the same doubts and lusts that I had to fight away every day.

After the service, Roger Prat came toward me. His eyes were again fastened on the cross around my neck, and he said, "Do you believe in destiny, William?"

I did not know how to reply, and he continued, "How did you come by this cross?"

"It belonged to my mother," I replied. "And she is dead."

Mistress Archard stood nearby, listening and nodding.

"But your mother," Prat continued, "taught you

to believe. She taught you that there are many ways of serving the Lord. Each man must find his way, isn't it so?"

I nodded, though I felt uncomfortable under his gaze.

"In this heathen land we're going to," said Prat, "I hear the savages hunger for the Word. Ignorant, like children, they must be taught. We cannot turn our faces away from them." He pointed his finger at me. "*Do* you believe in destiny?"

"Well, sir," I said haltingly, "I believe that some fine luck—er—some intervention made me come on this voyage. You see, I didn't know where to turn, and then I heard about. . . ."

"You were called," he interrupted, eyes blazing, "and you followed the call."

"He followed the call!" echoed Mistress Jones, who also stood listening.

Mistress Archard nodded, smiling warmly, her face serene. Suddenly I realized why she had chosen me to hold her baby, when to everyone else she had said, "No, thank you, but he wants his Mum." And I was filled with a strange mixture of feelings—a warm feeling of happiness, that these people were so ready to think well of me, to trust me; at the same time I felt guilty at having deceived them. I wanted to be everything they thought, devout and good and unselfish. And while they stood around me, smiling, I thought yes, maybe in the New World a person could make a new beginning.

* * *

"Poor little lost lamb, what's to become of it? Who's to save her when the time is near?"

"But you deceived me! If I'd have known. . . ."

Agnes Wood's laments, Ananais Dare's anger, Elinor Dare's sickness—it all came clear in a rush when the news spread among the passengers. Mistress Dare was with child.

Hugh, always alert to gossip, brought me the news. He'd gotten it from Brooke, who'd heard from Arnold Archard who'd been told by his wife.

"I knew it all along!" I blurted out, wanting to sound worldly. I told him all I'd overheard, and Hugh excitedly begged to hear more. We discussed it in great detail, that Elinor Dare had deceived her husband, that perhaps Governor White, too, had known and therefore had sent Ananais ahead to gather supplies. Between father and daughter, we said, there was this strange bond, "unhealthy bond," as Hugh put it. And we talked ourselves into foreboding. Between Governor White and Ananais Dare there existed a rift, which would widen, and then . . .

I was sorry afterward that I'd spoken. I liked them, all three. Why hadn't I kept still?

* * *

Day after day the same faces, the same complaints, the same people doing the very same things. The ship sailed on, on into the sunset, but it never really seemed to be getting anywhere because the sky was too vast, the ocean too wide.

I didn't realize it then, but it was on shipboard

that we truly became a colony. Together our moods changed, rose and fell like the swaying of the ship itself. One man and his wife would quarrel. Their grumbling would infect others. Soon the mood of irritation would spread into a general unrest. The weather became oppressive. We lay becalmed, scorching from the heat and glare. A listless mood hung over everyone. Then the wind blew again. Sails flapped and snapped, and a general sense of urgency arose. Let something happen! Anything!

We waited for it—whatever "it" was. Like Henry Rufoote, the bowing, bobbing little man who entertained us at night by telling the stars, we all began to look for signs and omens. Surely something would happen, something to show us why we had come so far from home. When "it" came, we would know immediately. We would say to ourselves, yes, I expected that all along—this is what the boredom has been leading to.

Even the sailors were restless, straining to sight another vessel. If it hoisted foreign colors, I knew they were ready for plundering, even for murder.

Uneasiness about our missing flyboat turned to alarm. Accusations against the Captain became bolder. Some of the men said that Captain Ferdinando had abandoned our flyboat deliberately. "How do you think King Philip is building that Armada of his?" Maurice Allen asked. "He's pirating every ship he can get his hands on."

"Come now," soothed Ananais. "What would he want with our little flyboat? Ferdinando's working for Raleigh. He's paid to deliver our fleet to the New World."

"I'd imagine the Spanish king pays even better for ships captured at sea and delivered to him."

After these conversations Hugh would tramp the length of the deck, glaring. "*Why* would Ferdinando forsake the flyboat?" It became a refrain.

I'd repeat what I'd overheard. "Listen, Ferdinando's English now. He's got himself an English wife. He's sailed for Raleigh before, and if Raleigh trusts him—don't mind what the others say. We'll probably meet the flyboat in the Indies."

But in my heart I kept thinking, "Beware of a man who laughs too much." And I was afraid.

SEVEN

OUR SUPPLY OF SALT was running low. "Never mind, never mind," came the word from the captain. "We'll soon sight land and take on salt aplenty."

We longed for land and solid ground, as much as we longed for meat. Like the sailors, we stood at the rail trying to distinguish new patterns and colors in the waves, designs that would show us that land was near. The men trimmed their hair and even their beards, waiting for something special. But nothing happened, only the same old quarrels and the waiting.

Accidents began to happen. Young Georgie Howe was hit by a spike that came loose in a wind storm. Emme Merrimoth and Margaret Lawrence tended him, arguing as he winced in pain.

"Dried mummy's the only thing!" Emme Merrimoth declared, forcing a pinch of it between the boy's teeth.

"Moss and sow bug!" Margaret argued. "I've worked in an apothecary shop, and I know!"

Bloodletting was the only remedy they agreed on. In the absence of a barber, Dr. Jones grudgingly performed bloodlettings. And he always had a large audience of people who wanted to learn how to do it.

"Come and watch, William," Hugh would coax. "You'd be good at it, you know. You already have a clever way with tools."

"I'd rather work with wood," I told Hugh. I'd watched once, and it turned my stomach.

"You'll have to get over this squeamishness," Hugh warned. Later I wished I had taken his advice.

Among those who watched every time were Tom Smart and the preacher's son, John Prat. It was taken for granted that John Prat was "a fine young man, about to follow in his father's footsteps." And he looked innocent enough, round faced, doffing his cap to everyone.

Ananais Dare particularly liked him, for he'd always rush to do as he was asked. "Yes, sir!" he'd say politely, and Ananais would murmur, "Fine young fellow." But John Prat was a liar, and I wondered why Ananais couldn't see it.

Roger Prat would ask his son what he'd been doing. "Oh, I've been studying my letters, Father," John would answer, his face glowing with virtue. "Up on deck I found a quiet place and studied these psalms as you said."

"Good, lad! We'll talk about it later together,"

his father would say, beaming.

But I'd know that all the while John had been sitting and listening to the sailors, whom he was forbidden to visit. Or he'd have been hanging over the edge fishing all morning, trying not for fish, but for gulls. He caught one once, hooked its mouth and let it be dragged half-dead behind the ship for hours.

In everything, Tom Smart was his shadow, his partner.

* * *

We had been on the high seas for forty days when the old mariners began to sniff the air, to lean far over the side, studying the colors and patterns of the waves.

At last came the cry from atop the mizzenmast, "Land ho!"

"Land ho!" echoed along the length of the ship, and not even the seasoned sailors remained unmoved at the sight. I felt most strongly then that man was never meant to live at sea. The island of Dominica lay before us like a living, throbbing thing, green and beautiful. Never before had I recognized the sweet scent of land or noticed its contours, or seen the infinite varieties of colors on a single hillside.

The little boys raced in circles and shouted, and the women's faces took on that quiet, shining look that women get when they are trying not to cry. Then they set about scrubbing their children and airing their clothes, and the widow Pierce brought out her precious paints and reddened her lips and cheeks.

We didn't weigh anchor, but rode alongside Dominica, then sighted Guadalupe. We sat up most of the night, too excited to sleep, and it seemed as if everyone had been saving something for this celebration. Glaven and Carrol sang old Irish songs, and George Howe played his mouth organ. And the tales they told! Emme Merrimoth, surrounded by listeners, lectured on plants and herbs and ultimately, poisons. The men spoke of hunting; Chris Cooper told high tales of daring on horseback, and George Howe spoke of quiet meadows and clear streams and the joy of stalking, for he was a huntsman by profession, and I've never seen a happier man.

" 'Twill be a hunter's paradise," he said, dreamily stroking his dog's head. "I've heard there are places where the hares leap out by the hundreds. I'll take you hunting, William," he said, "and then you'll see, there's no better life in all the world."

"And m-m-me t-too!" exclaimed his son.

"Certainly, Georgie! You'll have your own gun, and you and I will break new trails. What good times we'll have then!" he sighed, tousling his son's hair.

I tried not to stare at Georgie's crippled leg. His father didn't even seem to notice it, or the stammer that made the women shake their heads whenever the boy tried to speak.

From hunting, the talk went to savages, with

Chris Cooper stroking his sword and murmuring, "They make good hunting, I hear."

Maurice Allen, picking his teeth, recounted the death of the savage king Pemisipan, "A sight, let me tell you, to see that ugly savage head in the hands of our Irish boys! 'Twas cut in a single stroke, and you know, the savage kept on running, like a chicken that's lost its head."

"Do they bleed?" asked Berde, the farmer, wrinkling his brow.

"Of course!" said Maurice Allen with contempt. "Even a pig will bleed. But it's not the same," he said, cracking open a large nut. "Savage blood is thick and sluggish. It's what makes them slow and dull witted."

Elizabeth Glane, sitting close beside me, turned pale. "I should have stayed in Plymouth," she said. "Why did you let me come?" Her voice rose for everyone to hear, and I felt my face burning. "Why didn't you tell me about the savages?" she cried. "Oh, it was better in Plymouth; I should never have come! They'll catch me they will, and cook me in a pot!"

"Not you," cried Maurice Allen with a grin, "you're much too skinny, just a bag of bones. But look out you don't eat too much! They favor tasty young girls with a bit of flesh on 'em."

To my humiliation, she began to cry, and nothing I could say to soothe her made any difference. But George Howe came and put his hand on her shoulder. "Elizabeth," he said seriously, "William and I will look out for you. Do you think we'd let anyone harm you? Master Allen was only joking—a poor joke, to be sure. Why, if anyone had been eaten by savages, it would be he, for look how plump he is in the belly."

Elizabeth sniffed, wiped her nose on her sleeve and at last gave a wistful, crooked smile. But as soon as George had gone back to his playing, Elizabeth began again to twitch and sniffle. "Oh, William, I'm afraid! I should never have come!"

I looked at her thin grimy hands, the uneven, dirty hair, and I wondered that I could ever have compared her to Bessie, even for a moment.

"*Will* you take care of me?" her eyes seemed to say.

"I know what will make you feel better," I said, seeing that Henry Rufoote, bowing, was taking his leave from a group of men who'd been listening to his horoscopes. Dismayed, I approached him. It would cost me something—that I knew.

At my approach his wrinkled face broke into a smile. He bobbed several quick bows. "Yes, yes, and how may I be of service?"

"Elizabeth Glane is unhappy," I told him. "I thought maybe you could tell her—would tell the stars for her. I mean—if she were to hear something pleasant. . . . I mean—you can always find something pleasant to tell, can't you?"

He shrank back, deeply offended, and all the many lines in his face drew downward. "I can only tell what the stars reveal," he said sternly. "If you think that I am a scoundrel, an inventor of tales . . ."

"No, no," I said hastily. "What I meant was, I hope that you can cheer her—with your knowledge. Yes, with your wisdom, Master Rufoote. Because even if her destiny isn't—I mean, one ought to be prepared."

"Precisely," he said with another bow. "The stars do give warning, and if one is able to read the signs, sometimes he can avert . . ." His voice trailed off, and he looked at me with an intense expression. "Do you have any money?"

"No."

"What have you, then?"

"My humble skill," I replied, struggling not to smile. "I will carve you a set of spoons in exchange."

"Ah! A fine trade," he cried, bobbing and hurrying to Elizabeth.

Henry Rufoote held her entranced. He droned on and on, sometimes finishing his sentence, more often letting the thought trail away.

"Yes, it is all written clearly, your nature is bold, adventuresome—that is, you are the sort of woman who would. . . ."

"The best time for you is early spring, a time when decisions are made—good decisions. But you must not be hasty. You must not stray away from the path of. . . ."

"Your lucky number is seven, the same as the Governor's, if I may be so bold . . . and your unlucky number, on the other hand, is two."

Elizabeth smiled at him, and for a moment she

seemed almost womanly when she said, "Well, Master Rufoote, I won't do anything adventuresome or dangerous on days with the number two." Then she motioned him to come close and whispered something in his ear.

"Yes, indeed you will," he said in reply.

He left us, walking backward as was his custom. "What did you ask him?" I asked Elizabeth.

She smiled slightly. "It's a secret."

"Tell me. After all, I'm . . ."

"You're what?" she demanded.

"Never mind." I'd been about to retort that *I* was paying for it, but I said nothing more. A few moments later she was fast asleep, her head on my shoulder. I let her stay there. At least she wasn't talking or crying, so I let her stay. I guess I fell asleep too, for the next thing I knew everyone was running madly onto the deck, shouting, "Land! Santa Cruz! All ashore!"

The yeomen went ashore with sacks over their shoulders, hoping to find seedlings for transplanting in Virginia. The sailors rolled large kegs down the gangway, hoping to find fresh water. Elizabeth clutched my arm, hesitating and frightened, but also eager.

Margaret Lawrence walked with Chris Cooper and several others, and I heard her say, "Now, if only we can stay ashore for a time. If only the weather holds, and we don't meet any savages."

"The Captain says there are no savages here," Cooper replied, and Jane Jones, tugging at her white kerchief, echoed, "No savages."

"Perhaps the flyboat will meet us here!" Margaret continued. "Ah, if only we could all meet again."

If was her way. If the sun was shining she'd say, "If only it weren't so hot." If it grew cool she'd lament, "If only we had a bit of sun." Once I'd heard her muttering, "If only my hair weren't so *straight!*" Strange, the habit didn't annoy anyone. The men called her Lady Margaret, and they outdid one another in trying to please her, to make her world perfect.

No sooner had we stepped ashore, than we were stunned by the sight of five huge tortoises, sunning themselves in the sand. The huge beasts looked so awesome that we just stood for several minutes, gaping. Then someone shouted, "Meat!" and the chase was on.

"Just circle around slowly," shouted George Howe, but nobody paid any attention. Shrieking, running, hurling rocks and sticks, we descended upon the lumbering beasts like a wild mob. I lost myself in the wildness too, shouting and running, lunging after those tortoises as if my life depended upon it. Even the women shouted uncontrollably, though I wasn't aware of the screams until it was all over. Two of the beasts took to the water; soon the shallows were murky with their blood. I kept my eye on one of them that was struggling to clamber behind a boulder. Mine! It had to be mine! I could already taste it as I drew my knife, and I was filled with the lust for killing.

Just behind me John Sampson and his son came shouting and panting. But it was mine! Mine! They circled the boulder, trapping the tortoise, and with a cry of joy I plunged my knife into the beast's soft belly. Its legs shrank immediately into the shell, but its head hung out, and as it died it looked for all the world like a man with its wide, mocking slit of a mouth, twin holes for nostrils and those eyes—those tired, wounded eyes.

I felt giddy and weak. The muscles in my legs trembled, and I'd wrenched my shoulder in heaving the beast over on its side. But the prize was mine, a magnificent gigantic shell. It took fifteen men to drag my tortoise to the fire pits on the beach. And four men carried me, victorious, shouting and singing.

It was a glorious night for feasting, a Midsummer Night's Eve celebration three days early. Elizabeth sat apart with the women, for once, while I lay beside the fire with the men, savoring the cool night, the firm ground, the taste of fresh meat still in my mouth. The men came to clap me on the back, to say, "Well done, William! Splendid chase!"

It was good—good to sit among the men, to be one of them. George Howe brought out his mouth organ. Dyonis Harvie drummed on an empty keg with two sticks. Someone brought out a recorder, and they played "Greensleeves." Half-dreaming, I thought I smelled the scent of lavender.

Turning, I saw Margaret Lawrence beside me. She sat down on the sand without speaking, and I could see the pale silk of her hair gleaming in the firelight. And suddenly I was filled with desire.

"It was a good chase," she murmured, nodding toward the tortoiseshell. "didn't think you could be so—fierce."

I smiled, trying to think of something clever to say, but my head felt light. "I'm not usually—unless I want something badly."

"And does that happen often?"

"Not often, but when it does . . ."

"Then you find a way to get what you want," she finished for me.

The others seemed to fade to a distance, but the heat from the fire was scorchingly near, as near as Margaret Lawrence with her scent of lavender and silky hair brushing my arm.

"What are you going to do with the tortoiseshell?" she asked.

"I'm not sure," I replied. My heart was beating frantically. I'd give her the tortoiseshell polished like marble, anything . . .

There was a cry. "William! William!" Elizabeth came stumbling toward me. Her fists were dug into her eyes. White foam oozed from her lips.

"What did you do?" I shouted, shaking her. "What did you eat? Spit it out!"

"Apples, just apples!" she cried. "I'm poisoned. I'll *die*. I can't see."

* * *

We brought her back to the ship, along with a dozen or so others who had eaten the poisonous fruit or drunk the putrid water. They writhed and wailed and pleaded for the doctor. "Take her below!" Dr. Jones shouted to me. "I'll come when I can."

"I'll tend to her," said Margaret, grasping Elizabeth's arm. "Hush! Stop that wailing," she commanded, but Elizabeth only kicked and cursed.

I glimpsed Emme Merrimoth coming aboard, calling out, "Now! Now you'll need me!" But I shrugged her aside and retorted, "There are plenty of others." With a fierce look she hobbled over toward Joyce Archard and the baby that lay at her breast, screaming.

"Fetch some water," Margaret commanded, when we had laid Elizabeth down on the bunk. "Keep wiping her while I get my things."

She hurried away, then returned with a satchel. "Lucky I have a bit of bezoar stone already powdered," she said briskly. She put it into my tin cup, mixed it with water and forced the liquid between Elizabeth's lips.

"You're choking me, you bitch!" screamed Elizabeth, thrashing wildly. "Don't touch me, you filthy daughter of a. . . ."

With a calm but determined air Margaret told me, "Go get someone. We'll have to let blood, and quickly, before the poison spreads."

"You'll get no blood out of me!" screamed Elizabeth, striking out with her fists.

Up on deck, amid the awful confusion, I found Dyonis Harvie, tending his wife. "Can you come? Elizabeth . . ." I stammered.

"Get one of the others," Harvie shouted back.

"Who?"

"Brooke."

But Brooke was already surrounded by patients, as were the goldsmith and all the others who now plied their new trade as surgeons.

I rushed back to Dyonis Harvie. "Please!" I begged. "Come now, before the poison spreads."

"You can do it," he said, glancing up at me. "Look." He pointed his knife at his wife's arm. "Make a cut—here—about so deep. You'll manage. Do you have a knife?"

I nodded, clutching at my stomach, for while he spoke Harvie pressed the blade into his wife's forearm, then turned it to let the blood pour onto the deck.

Below again, I called to Margaret. "Nobody will come. You have to do it. Have you ever? . . ."

"Not I," she said firmly. "Bloodletting is man's work."

"I can't! I can't!"

"You were so brave with the tortoise! You'll see, it's just the same."

"Don't touch me!" screamed Elizabeth, kicking and turning.

"You'll have to hold her down," I said grimly, and Margaret pinned down Elizabeth's arms, bracing her knee on Elizabeth's stomach. "Now," she commanded. "Cut."

I tried once, twice, but the knife simply wouldn't go in.

"Damn you, *press!*" shouted Margaret.

I pressed, Elizabeth screamed, and then she fainted.

"I see your patient is resting well!" called Dr. Jones. He peered at Elizabeth from a distance. "Ah, she's fainted. Just as well. The poison burns the mouth. It's quite amazing," he continued thoughtfully. "Even Mistress Archard's baby is afflicted, took in the poison from its mother's milk."

I wanted to scream at him, for Elizabeth looked as pale and still as if she were dead, and the bleeding still hadn't stopped. But, controlling my temper, I asked him, "What shall we do?"

"Press a bit of cloth over the wound. And, she ought to take some—ah, a bit of—"

"Crocodile blood?" ventured Margaret with a smile.

"Precisely. Yes, it will strengthen her liver. It is essential."

Margaret faced me triumphantly. "Tomorrow you must go ashore and find a crocodile."

My supper seemed to be churning in my chest, rising to my mouth. I? *I* must find a crocodile? *I* must let blood? *I* must be ordered around by everyone and his brother, told what to do, when to do it? I'd come away for freedom!

"Very well," I said meekly. The next morning I went ashore. After hours of searching behind every rock and shrub on that blasted beach, I finally caught a small reptile. I didn't know whether it was a large lizard or an infant crocodile. Anyway,

Margaret was satisfied. She squeezed out its blood and powdered some skin for good measure. Still, Elizabeth didn't get well.

Of all who had been taken sick, Elizabeth was the worst. The others had regained their sight, and their sores were beginning to fade. But after five days and nights. Elizabeth only grew thinner and more restless. Then she fell into a steady sleep that frightened me even more.

Roger Prat came to stand over her, reciting a prayer.

"It is God's will," he told me reverently.

And I thought, yes, maybe she will die, and I will be free again, and it's all God's will. When I came near, she awakened and grasped my hand, called my name. And I felt a huge wave of tenderness and remorse. I didn't want her to die.

"Pray!" I told Roger Prat, and I closed my eyes in prayer. But still Elizabeth did not get well.

Then Emme Merrimoth came. She waddled over, gray hair standing out, and I took off my cap in greeting.

"So, do you have need of me yet, pretty William?"

It was what she always called me, in that half-mocking tone of hers.

"I beg your help," I said humbly, nodding toward Elizabeth.

"Ah, it's easy to beg," she crooned. "Words are cheap."

"If you could cure her . . ."

"You'll make me a fine chest," Emme Merrimoth said. "A *fine* chest with three drawers, perhaps of cedar. I've heard that the cedars of Virginia are taller than the cedars of Lebanon!"

"Yes, yes," I agreed, and stood back to let her examine Elizabeth.

With her finger she pried open Elizabeth's mouth and looked inside. She peered into her nostrils, felt her face all over. "Yes," she muttered, "I can do it." Then, tottering back and forth beside the bunk, she bent her head and mumbled a chant about fire, water, blazing and burning. Lastly she stood over Elizabeth, cleared her throat and spat squarely in her face.

"What—*what?*" I shouted, outraged.

"She'll recover now," said Emme Merrimoth. "You'll see."

It was true. By the next morning Elizabeth's fever had broken. She lay quietly and even took a cup of gruel. In a few days she was herself again, following me around more closely than ever.

* * *

Something evil was bound to happen, but I think we all tried not to see it. Of course we knew—had to know that something was wrong. I don't know what the others thought in private; but more and more often, when the Captain was quite alone in his cabin, I heard him laughing. And I felt terrible premonitions, though I didn't say anything to anybody. We were all intent on telling each other that everything was all right, that we were in good hands with Ferdinando, and not to worry.

By now our salt was almost gone. Grain was running out. Why wouldn't the Captain stop as he'd promised? And where would we get the cattle we'd need to survive the winter in Virginia?

The Captain had promised we'd find fresh water aplenty at Santa Cruz. In searching for it our men spent more beer than they found water, bringing back only two bottles.

"Well then, we'll take on water at Cottea," we told each other. "The Captain needs water as much as we do, doesn't he?"

Again, at Cottea, there was no water to be had. And on the Island of Beake, where we'd stopped to buy sheep, there were none.

"Be assured," came word from the Captain, "we'll find salt at Mosquitos Bay."

But when the time came, we stopped only long enough to let Glaven and Carrol ashore.

Some of the men still grumbled, but softly, while glancing over their shoulders. They told each other, "The Captain's in a hurry to land us, to do a bit of privateering on the way home." They cursed him and hated him for it, but it was customary, after all, for sea captains to take a bit of plunder.

But none ever said any more, "The Captain doesn't want our colony to succeed. He'll get us there, but without provisions." None ever said, "Can't you see it? He's in league with King Philip, the treacherous Spanish dog! Forsook our flyboat, didn't he, and God, they're probably captured and dead by now."

Nobody said these things, because we were part of this ship, and the ship was ruled by Ferdinando. Nobody, not even our Governor, could change that.

So we lied to ourselves and each other, and when we sighted San Juan, two dozen men stood on the deck with salt sacks slung over their shoulders. The farmers stood ready to go ashore for cattle and seedlings. Again the water casks were rolled out. And we waited. We neared the shore, smelled the fragrance of trees and flowers, already felt the joy and relief of finding solid ground under our feet.

"You see!" cried Ananais. "We'll take on everything we need now. And it's beautiful here! Much better than Beake or Cottea. Captain says we might lay over for a week—a whole week!"

We were in a high good humor, laughing and joking, ready to go ashore.

But what meant that swirling foam just ahead of us? Those rocks, like lagged claws, that water dark and broiling. . . .

"The Captain says you'd best remain on board!" shouted the bosun, pushing his way toward Governor White. "This is not the place he thought."

"On–on board?" echoed the Governor, stunned.

"The coast is bristling with rocks. See? Look, there!"

I felt only a single lunge, heard the Captain's frantic screams, "Bear up! Bear up hard! By God, you'll wreck her on the reefs!"

The ship seemed to buckle under us, and from

somewhere came a great roar, ripping splintering sounds, and I felt myself hurled up and up, then down into darkness.

* * *

I awakened with a terrible taste in my mouth and some evil-smelling poultice under my nose. Over me stood Emme Merrimoth, and Elizabeth beside her looked at me with anxious, frightened eyes. "You fell and hit your head," she whispered.

Meekly I thanked Mistress Merrimoth for whatever it was she'd done to me. "No charge," she said cheerfully and waddled away.

My head felt double its size, and my mouth was dry. I lay back, wanting only to sleep, but Elizabeth began to whisper urgently.

"I was out on deck this morning," she whimpered. "William! I heard them talking. They won't take us. They'll leave us on Roanoke, and the savages will. . . ."

"For God's sake, what are you babbling about!" I raised myself on one elbow and felt a stab of pain in my head. Groaning, I fell back. "Go away," I said.

"No! I heard the sailors talking. They're going to leave us on Roanoke! That's the dreadful place— didn't you hear? How savages run with their heads cut off?" She began to cry, and I tried desperately to clear my head.

"Why were you up on deck alone, anyway?"

"I heard them. . . ."

"Come now," I soothed her. "Don't take on. Soon we'll be landing at Haiti, and we'll get all our supplies there. Sailors have nothing to say about where we land. We're ordered to go to Chesapeake. Raleigh himself has ordered it. We'll land on Roanoke only long enough to fetch back our Englishmen. You probably heard it wrong," I continued. "You were excited and afraid from the storm."

"And you—you being hurt!"

"But everything is all right now," I said, and finally she was calm again.

The next day we rode with the coast of Hispaniola, waiting any moment to put ashore. But hours passed. The sun began to sink. The Captain did not appear on deck. He sent a brief message. "Tomorrow."

The Captain had told Governor White and Ananais Dare that on Haiti he knew a man called Alanson, who would supply us with everything we needed. Well then, this was what we had waited for—perhaps Ferdinando had arranged it all along, to trade with his friend, Alanson.

But in the afternoon of the next day we knew we had passed the port of Haiti. The Captain appeared among us, shouting, "Dead! That scoundrel Alanson is dead! We sail on, to Virginia!"

EIGHT

CAPE FEAR. When sailors say the name, they quickly cross themselves, then speak of something else. We were nearly wrecked on the rocks of Cape Fear.

But then, then came the beautiful calm after the storm, as if the sea were trying to make up for the terror of the night. Gently, calmly *The Lion* slipped into the harbor at Hatorask, with the pinnace bobbing merrily alongside. We saw the lush growth. We smelled the sweet vines and flowers and fruits. Virginia! We were almost home.

Most of us would not go ashore. The Governor chose only forty men to carry out the rescue mission. Richard Berry assembled them on the deck, barking out instructions. Then suddenly he roared out my name. "Wythers! Go tell the Governor we stand ready!"

I hurried to Governor White's cabin and found

him bent over our trumpeter, who lay limp and grinning in a corner.

"The men are assembled, sir!" I gave the message.

Governor White glanced up, frowning. Then eagerly he asked, "William, can you blow a trumpet?"

I stood dumbly, astounded.

"Just a note or two will do. It seems our trumpeter drowned his sorrows in rum last night. He can hardly stand, much less blow a note. Here!" He took up the instrument and gave it to me. "Give it a try. Just a blast—a noise to summon our countrymen!"

"I'll try, sir," I said, taking up the trumpet. It would mean that I, too, would go ashore! I put the trumpet to my lips. Out came a squawk like a wounded rooster, and the Governor sank down with laughter.

"You can practice a bit," he told me. "Then come ashore with us."

By the time the pinnace was brought alongside, ready for us to board her, I was able to blow a fairly respectable long note, followed by a short toot.

"You do have the strangest way of getting into the middle of things!" exclaimed Hugh. I could see the envy in his eyes. He hadn't been chosen to go ashore, though he'd been talking about it all night.

"You might need something," he said, unbuckling his sword.

"Oh, I don't think . . ." I began.

"Take it," he insisted. "It's no use to me here," he added gloomily.

"But I don't even know how . . ."

"Just thrust it out," he replied. "You've mown hay, haven't you? It's the same—whack! That's all. The sword does the rest."

It felt strange and grand, awkward and wonderful around my waist. Again and again I gripped the hilt, pretending to myself that I had to draw quickly. Elizabeth caught me at my playacting and said scornfully, "Oh, so you fancy yourself a soldier!"

"We'll see," I said loftily, "when I return. Perhaps I'll just come back with a trophy in my hand."

"P'raps he will," cackled Maurice Allen. "He might just catch a savage and cut off his . . ."

"Company! Forward. . . ."

We boarded the pinnace, and as we moved out I looked back at *The Lion*. Her bow seemed huge, and her cannon bristled. From the deck our friends waved and called good luck. Then we could no longer see their faces or hear their voices. All around me the soldiers were talking and laughing, like sportsmen excited before a hunt. By contrast, the silence from the flagship, the slowed-down movements of faceless figures on the deck, seemed eerie and almost menacing.

"They're manning the cannons for us," Richard Berry remarked to the Governor, "in case the savages try something."

"But we're well armed," Governor White objected. "Our forty best soldiers. . . ."

I glanced at Ananais Dare. His face was damp with sweat. I wanted to talk to him, to find out whether anyone else felt as I did, the dread and the longing for action. My breathing was fast; my shirt was soaked, and all I could think of was how my knife had sunk into the belly of that tortoise, how this sword at my side might soon sink into the belly of a savage.

Our sailors were quiet and sullen; they spoke only with each other. Then they stopped talking altogether, seeming to communicate with their grim, set faces, and with their eyes. The same silence settled over the soldiers, as if a signal had been given, and they all knew the proper pose for this moment.

I followed their example, moving quickly, silently down to the shore. The soldiers stood in silent formation, while Richard Berry scanned the beach. We would search all day and return to the flagship at dusk. The search would continue every day, until Grenville's men were found, alive or dead. And every day I would walk behind our soldiers, sounding the trumpet.

A signal passed between the muster captain and the Governor, who stood with me, nearest the shore. "Sound the trumpet!" shouted the Governor, and I gave a sharp blast.

Now the column moved out, and I had taken only a few steps when the mate strode up to the Governor.

"Orders from Captain Ferdinando!" said the mate. He stood at attention, and though he faced the Governor squarely, he was looking beyond him, as men do when they deliver such messages. "We are ordered to leave your searching party here on Roanoke. The flagship will weigh anchor at high noon. Captain Ferdinando says that the Governor himself may return to the flagship if he wishes, but with only two or three of his soldiers. Captain Ferdinando says the others are forbidden to return to the ship."

"Forbidden!"

"My orders, sir. Does the Governor wish to return to the flagship?"

The column of soldiers moved over the crest of a hill. A volley of signal shots rang out.

Without a trace of emotion the Governor snapped back at the mate, "You may take me to the Captain now." He turned to me. "Come with me, William. I may need you as a messenger."

All the way back to the flagship the Governor's face bore that look of stern composure. He spoke only once, more to himself than to me, saying, "Well, now we know."

Captain Ferdinando stood leaning against the rail, waiting, watching our approach.

The colonists were gathered aft, held there by the posture and position of the sailors.

I could see a muscle in Governor White's throat throbbing, as he addressed the Captain. "Captain Ferdinando, I've been told that my searchers are to remain on Roanoke. I would like to remind the Captain that . . ."

"The summer is far spent," said the Captain. Suddenly his face looked pinched and drawn; it seemed impossible that he had ever laughed, or ever would again.

"Captain, I can see no reason why we shouldn't proceed with our plans." The Governor's voice was firm, but it also had a soothing, coaxing quality, as if he were addressing an unreasonable child.

"Sailors," said the Captain, "are a superstitious lot. They think that our close encounter at Cape Fear was a bad omen."

"But surely," said Governor White, "the Captain won't be swayed by the superstitions of the crew."

"The sailors speak from experience. The summer is far spent, and . . ."

"It's only July!"

"And they are eager to return to England. Unfortunately, precious time was lost hunting for seedlings and such. The ship is sorely in need of repair."

"Then lay over here for repairs, while we search for our men, and then sail us on to Chesapeake."

"You fail to understand, Governor White. To make this ship fit for her return voyage will take a month at least. God only knows how long it would take, in our battered condition, to reach Chesapeake. 'Tis miracle enough that we landed safe here, what with the maze of inlets and the treacherous winds. Not one of us has sailed to Chesapeake before—but though my men are weary and afraid, we will sail, yes! today, if the Governor wishes."

"And leave my soldiers stranded on Roanoke!"

"Or we can land your colonists on Roanoke Island."

Stiffly now the Governor said, "May I remind the Captain that Sir Walter Raleigh's written orders command us first to rescue Grenville's men, then to plant our colony at Chesapeake."

"In a situation like this, Governor, the Captain's judgment stands above written orders." Ferdinando moved his hand slightly. Immediately a dozen crew members were beside him.

"My first duty," said Ferdinando loudly, "is the safe return of this ship and my crew. You must decide, Governor. Which will it be? Roanoke or Chesapeake?"

A flush rose to the Governor's face, but his inner struggle lasted only a moment. "I will not forsake my countrymen," he shouted. "Relief has been promised Grenville's men. We will not abandon them. And I will not leave my soldiers here without supplies and split our colony into two parts. We will land on Roanoke and take our chances on reaching Chesapeake in the spring—with the help of the Almighty."

* * *

When we went ashore on Roanoke Island, our landing was far different from what I'd imagined it would be. I had dreamed of it as a glorious time, when the Governor would lead us in proud procession to claim the land, then together we would pray in gratitude and awe.

But we came down from the ship weary and

beaten, ragtag and dirty, sullen and angry. Long afterward I still heard echoes of the rowdy, surly mob we had become.

"It's because of the women. Women on voyages are always bad luck."

"All they want is a roof over their heads, a place to give birth to their brats!"

"Our Governor considers the welfare of his daughter more important than the success of the colony! We were promised a landing at Chesapeake!"

"Chesapeake!" they shouted. I glanced at the faces of the men I'd come to know during the voyage, utterly changed now. Their faces were bloated with anger. And I heard Mistress Viccars saying, "We should have known there'd be no wealth for the likes of us. Promises, that's all we'll ever get."

The shouting stopped only when Governor White fired a shot into the air. He was no longer mild and gentle. Fiercely he looked down at the colonists from the small knoll where he stood beside the standard he had planted there. "Silence!" he roared. "I rule here in the name of the Queen! I warn you, we will not begin our new lives here in anarchy."

Behind him the forty soldiers had gathered, weapons ready, and beside him stood all the Assistants, even Christopher Cooper who had been among the rabble.

"You made your decision when you came on this venture!" the Governor shouted. "But any of you who haven't got the stomach to see it through, can go back to England with our ships. Step forward then, now, and be counted."

Nobody moved. The silence was complete. For many minutes the colonists stood, eyes downcast. At last the Governor spoke again, this time in his accustomed calm tone.

"Very well," he said. "We stand united. I have lived here on Roanoke," he said gently, "and I tell you, it is a goodly land. We can live here in peace until spring. We must prepare our fort and plant and lay in supplies for winter. We will not spend our energy warring with savages or hunting for treasure. And in the spring," he said, "we will move to Chesapeake, and we will form the town to be called Raleigh, Virginia, the first permanent English town in the New World. This island of Roanoke," he said with a wide gesture, "will be our testing ground."

And now Roger Prat did lead us in prayer. He spoke passionately of the Israelites who had wandered in the desert for forty years before they were led to the promised land.

"Give us strength, oh merciful God, and courage, that we may be worthy to claim this new promised land called Chesapeake. Grant us patience, until in spring, united in spirit and tempered by this trial, we emerge worthy to receive Thy blessing."

Subdued now, the colonists spoke in gentle tones.

"The Governor is right. It would have been dishonorable to betray our countrymen."

"Chesapeake in spring! The gold will still be there."

"And the pearls. They say there's a great river of pearls. . . ."

Elizabeth only looked at me and said, "I told you so."

Part Two

NINE

"OH, LOOK! Look! There's one behind the bush, a small one. Isn't it cunning? Naked as a starling."

"Three of them. Look, how the bigger one holds the baby on its back."

"Ambrose, you stay right here. Don't go any closer. You never know what sort of . . ."

"Naked as a starling," echoed Mistress Jones, pursing her lips. "And isn't it strange we've seen no big ones?"

Jane Pierce held out her hand, on which her rings gleamed. "Come here," she said sweetly, kneeling. "Come, see the pretty rings."

But the three brown-skinned savage children in the clearing only stared at us. Elizabeth, tugging at my arm, urged me to stop working. "Look! Aren't they cunning?"

"They'll come around of their own accord," said

George Howe pleasantly. "Don't rush them."

"Come on," coaxed Mistress Pierce, wriggling her fingers, but the children only stared. The older girl, with the baby on her back, must have been about five or six. She regarded us solemnly with large, curious eyes. The little boy beside her, naked and potbellied, clutched his hands over his stomach and his mouth turned downward in fright.

"Strange little creatures," said Mistress Viccars, keeping a firm grasp on Ambrose's hand. "I hear their village is just beyond that grove of trees. Why haven't they come out before?"

"They're afraid of us," replied Jane Pierce, "and it's no wonder, the way our soldiers are tramping through and firing shots into the air."

Without the slightest sound or signal between them, the children suddenly ducked down behind the bushes and were gone.

"Do you think their parents just set them out like that?" asked Mistress Viccars. "I mean, do you suppose they've got to grub for their own food?"

"I'll go catch one," cried Tom Smart, but George Howe caught him by the shirttail and said, "Let's go get some fresh water, Tom. The men will soon be coming back for lunch."

"Best stay away from them," added Mistress Viccars, "until we know. . . ."

"Best stay away from them!" Mistress Jones echoed sharply, unwrapping several cold biscuits for her husband's lunch.

"Come and eat, William!" Elizabeth said, and

though I was hungry, I paused to pull up several more handfuls of wild melon stalks. "Those small ones don't look a bit dangerous," Elizabeth continued excitedly. "Wouldn't it be nice if they could talk?"

"I'm sure they can talk," I said, stretching to ease the ache in my back.

It was our second day on Roanoke Island, and we'd been working since sunup to clear out the old fort. We had slept last night amid the ruins, using fallen logs for pillows, the women trying to pretend that the crumbling cabins with their torn roofs and overgrown dirt floors really did provide shelter.

Only the soldiers ventured away from the site of Lane's old fort. Governor White had ordered the rest of us to begin repairing the buildings. Only eight small huts were still standing, and these were in various stages of ruin. Ananais and John Sampson kept us going at a run. Somehow we would have to create a village here before winter.

Hugh squatted down beside me with a grunt. "Any word from the Governor?" he asked, nodding all around.

"He's still questioning Manteo," said Brooke.

"Did you see him, William?" Hugh asked.

"Just a glance. I hadn't thought they were so— tall." It wasn't at all what I'd meant to say. I'd caught a glimpse of him last night, tall and straight as any man, and even smiling. His appearance was so different from my many visions of savages that I still hadn't gotten over it.

"How can the Governor talk to him?" Elizabeth exclaimed. "*Does* he talk? What sort of language? . . ."

"Talks English," said Brooke, laughing. "You ought to hear it! Now, there's a sight for you to picture, that savage, half-naked, mind you, sitting on a satin cushion right in the palace, speaking English with her highness, meeting noblemen the likes of which you'd never see in a lifetime."

"If he speaks so well," said Maurice Allen sharply, "he'll be able to tell us what happened to Grenville's men. They haven't found hide nor hair of 'em, and no bones either."

"Very likely they're dead," said Joyce Archard, wrapping her baby more tightly.

"Now, Joyce," said her husband, wiping his face, "you mustn't always look for the worst."

"I'll look for the worst and be pleasantly surprised, thank you!" she snapped, jostling the baby over her shoulder. "Sit down, Arnold," she added more gently. "You're all flushed and hot."

He sat down with a sigh. "I didn't come to be a farmer, but," he shrugged, "it seems the Governor's decided we're all peasants." He held out his hands, stained green, like mine.

"We're all the same here," said Maurice Allen, grinning. "We're all going to get our hands blistered."

"What about you, then?" asked Brooke. "I haven't seen you moving any logs or clearing out rocks."

"Every job needs a supervisor," said Allen

cheerfully. "And my constitution isn't what it ought to be."

"Whose is?" I said. "I spent half of yesterday behind the bushes . . . begging your pardon," I added hastily, as Mistress Archard gave me a stern frown. "This morning I walked into that hut over there, and you know what I saw? Deer. Deer inside, feeding on the wild melon. All in a year's time, and the whole floor was choked with them."

"If only we could eat them," said Margaret Lawrence. "I suppose the savages do."

"If only it weren't so beastly hot!"

"We'll have to cut a road here. . . ."

"First thing, we'll have to mend those walls. Can't just live out here in the open."

"Ananais says we don't need a wall."

"A lot he knows! I'd rather those savages would come and show themselves. You can feel them creeping about, staring."

"Well, Manteo's come out. D'you know what he told the Governor? Said he'd been at his home on Croatoan all winter, but he had a vision. Fancy it, a vision! Said he got a vision to come to Roanoke, to meet us."

"If he's so good at visions, let him tell us what happened to Grenville's men. God, but it's beastly hot!"

All day we heard the sounds of the searching party's trumpet calls echoing from the hills. It was always the same four notes, never the signal, "they are found."

Nobody else seemed confused. But all the second day I kept waiting for someone to tell me what to do, where to go. Most of the time I simply followed the others, my mind dazed, my body numb. I recalled Master Taylor's words, "Can you imagine wilderness?" and I had to close my eyes against it. It was too strange, too sudden. Thus I seemed to fall into a kind of wakeful sleep, a stupor, only half seeing the peculiar shrieking birds, the towering trees, the ground laced and interlaced with shrubs and blossoms of such variety that I had no words to describe them.

I followed the others, ate the meager meals someone cooked from our ship's stores, made my bed under a tree as I had the night before, and fell asleep. It was a deep sleep, like death or fever. The next morning, when I awakened to the impatient tapping of a woodpecker, saw the sun slanting between the leaves, felt the hard ground under me, at first I couldn't collect my thoughts.

Strange, unrelated memories came upon me, then terrible questions flooded my mind. It was like that for several days. While I was working, or with the others, I felt quite myself. But as soon as I stopped, or when I was alone, those terrible questions would return. "Where am I? What am I doing here? Why have I come?" And then I would realize, "This is the New World," and I would hear an echo of Governor White's words, which I'd accepted so easily while sitting in his house in London, "From Virginia, there is no other place to go."

I worked harder than I'd ever done, patching roofs, mending walls, helping Ananais to build walkways and fire pits. I clung to my fellow colonists, leaving the group only for those moments that I needed the bushes. The least comment from someone I'd hardly spoken to before, loosed a stream of talk from me. I talked to Berde the farmer about grain, as if my life depended upon it. Hynde, the thief, whom I'd carefully ignored on shipboard, worked beside me patching a roof, and as we hammered we talked—about flowers, of all things—wild flowers! He planned to press out their nectar to make a new kind of wine, and we discussed it at length.

But when he'd climbed down from the roof, and I was alone, again came the troublesome thoughts. "Where am I? What am I doing here? From Virginia there is no other place to go."

Just after supper the third day, John Brooke approached me. He'd been eying me, rocking back on his heels, half smiling. "Don't worry about it, William," he said kindly, as if he'd read my thoughts. "It only lasts a few days."

I stared up at him. "What do you mean?"

"These strange feelings. Your body humors are not yet in tune with the elements. Everything is different here—the air, the water, the earth itself."

"I feel all turned around," I admitted, and admitting it, a heaviness rose to my chest.

"It will pass," he assured me.

"If I only knew—the sea is there, due east, but

what's beyond those trees? And at the edge of Roanoke Island—what is there?" I tried to sound calm, but my voice betrayed my great sense of urgency. If only I could know the names of the places nearby, what to expect, what kinds of distances existed, what manner of people!

John Brooke squatted down beside me and took up a long stick. In the sand he drew a nearly round circle. "This is Roanoke," he said, pointing. "Here, all around it, are the waters of Pamlico Sound. East, beyond the Sound, of course, is the Atlantic Ocean."

I nodded, squinting down at the marks in the sand.

"The Sound," he continued, "is enclosed by four islands." He drew four shapes stretching from north to south. "The first, opposite Roanoke, is called Hatorask. It's shaped like a long arm, bent at the elbow. Below it is another long arm. The natives call it Paquiwok. Then comes Croatoan—Manteo's home, then a much smaller island called Wokokon."

"But where's Chesapeake?" I cried.

"Here, west from Roanoke, on the mainland, then north. The mainland is vast, very vast, William. I don't know the names of many towns, but I've heard of Pomiock and Secota, and that Secota is very green, very beautiful. Now, to come to Chesapeake, we'll cross the water, here to an Indian town called Dasamonquepeuk. Then we'll move north through many other towns, many days' walk, until we come to a great river. There lies Chesapeake."

"I'll never remember it all!" I exclaimed.

"You will," he said. "Why not write it down?"

I had no paper. I thanked John Brooke and set out, for the first time away from the others, and the ground did not feel so strange under my feet. I repeated the foreign-sounding names to myself, then turned to find some paper, irritated that I'd have to beg even for that.

I went to the largest of the cabins, which was to be occupied by the Governor and Ananais and Elinor Dare.

"Come in, William!" she called as I stood in the doorway. "There's no door yet to knock on," she added, laughing, "so we can't be formal."

I stepped onto the dirt floor, which had been swept amazingly clean and smooth. One wall of the hut was entirely knocked out. But in the middle of the room stood a bedstead, complete with posts and coverlets. In this broken, dismal hut it looked so forlorn, but at the same time so comical, that I felt caught between laughter and pity. And Agnes Wood stood at the window hanging a curtain!

What are we doing here? For a moment I felt dizzy. Elinor Dare, with her red hair done up, her bright smile and a blue checked dress, looked like a young girl playing at housekeeping.

"Sit down a while," she said softly. "You look tired." She pointed to an empty barrel and sat down opposite me on a rickety chair. "You've come for news, I suppose," she said, "and my father isn't here, nor is Ananais."

I felt a certain warmth at the words "my father," for in company, she usually referred to him formally as "the Governor."

"What news?" I asked, pulling myself up straight.

"Well, Manteo assures us that the natives want to live in peace with us," she began, looking down at her hands. They were white and slender, and I wondered how long they would stay that way. She must have caught my glance, for quickly she curled her thumb under her fingers, concealing a ragged nail.

"Is Manteo a leader of the Roanoke natives?" I asked, using her term instead of "savages."

"No. He's from Croatoan, but I suppose he has some influence here. His father is a great chief in a province some distance from here. It's called Chawanook, I think. Anyway, Manteo has talked to the Roanoke people, and apparently they are peaceable. But there's a band—a group led by Wanchese, that he can't vouch for."

"Wanchese—that other one they brought to England?"

"Yes. Apparently Wanchese was a great friend and follower of Pemisipan, the chief who was killed. Now Wanchese is the leader of a renegade group, followers of Pemisipan and some other warriors. They call themselves Wingos."

"So, I suppose Wanchese plans to avenge Pemisipan's death," I said.

Elinor nodded. "My husband says we've nothing to fear. They're just a small band—outcasts, really. And we're well armed."

There was a ripping sound as Agnes Wood opened another crate, then came to ask, "What shall I do with the dishes, Mistress?"

"Just leave them in the crate, Agnes," she replied. "I'll have to see about getting some shelves."

I stood up. "I'd be happy to help," I offered.

Elinor Dare's smile almost made me forget the reason for my call, but then I remembered the paper, and she went to fetch some for me.

"About the shelves," I began.

"Oh, anyone can make shelves," she said. "I'll have some of the boys work on that. But," she added, smiling again, "if it isn't too much trouble, there is something very special I'll need." She lowered her voice almost to a whisper. "A cradle."

As I left the cottage, I found myself smiling, filled with a sense of belonging. It was only when I saw our night sentinels station themselves for duty on the hills that I remembered we were in the wilderness, perhaps being watched by unseen savages who hungered for revenge.

* * *

"Miracle of God!"

The calling of our sentinels echoed from the hills.

"Miracle of God! Our ship! Our flyboat is in the harbor!"

We ran to the beach. It was true. We laughed and wept, shouted and embraced old friends, and prayed. "Miracle! Miracle of God!" Our flyboat had landed, and all were safe.

But in the midst of our rejoicing, even as I

embraced Clement Taylor, I saw Ferdinando's face and felt a blinding anger. Had we all gone mad? Were our memories so short? If any further proof of treachery were needed, the look on Ferdinando's face told it all.

But Captain Spicer strode up to Ferdinando jovially. "Ferdinando! You left a trail for us on the water, eh? Unfortunately we lost you, but no matter. The Lord made His heavens to guide us."

"You passed no vessels on the way?"

"Not one. 'Twas a bit lonely, to be sure, but here we are, and not a mite too soon. She'll need a good bit of trimming. She's held together with spit and a prayer."

Even Hugh seemed to have forgotten his anguish on shipboard, as exuberantly he punched and patted his brother and rushed to tell everything at once.

My anger was so strong that I moved away from them, and I heard the Governor speaking to Sampson and Ananais. He had not forgotten. He would not forgive. I heard him say in a trembling voice, "Rest assured, I will make a full written report about this to Sir Walter Raleigh."

"Of course, you must," agreed Ananais Dare, and Sampson nodded.

I could picture Ferdinando roaring with laughter, flicking his wrist and saying, "May it please you!"

There would be no justice.

TEN

THE OLD FORT was separated from the native village by a fine, thick stand of cedar and pine. We did not venture across this barrier, but every day more of the little brown-skinned children slipped out of the grove to stare at us, then to disappear again noiselessly. From the grove Manteo would emerge to bring us berries, strings of freshly caught fish and fowl.

For several days I only watched him—curious, puzzled, afraid of his darkness. The more I watched him the more I wondered—what made him so strange? How well he concealed his wildness! Would he lash out suddenly, like a baited bear? Roger Prat spoke a great deal about the absent souls of the savages. "They are seeking and searching— they have only us to show them the Way." We were seeing the shapes and figures of men, Prat told us, but with something still missing. Furtively I'd steal glances at Manteo, envisioning him empty inside, like a figure made of wax.

When he was gone I would picture him. He was sleek and smooth and his muscles seemed to roll when he moved. What caused that strange, immobile expression he usually wore? And who had taught him to laugh? I had heard that savages did not know how to laugh.

As I pondered, I began to explore the island, going off late in the afternoon when the day's work was done. One day I found myself a very special place.

At the northern end of the island, a good distance from our fort, a steep palisade of crags and cliffs rose up from the shore. Approaching from the landward side, the hill was gentle at first, then ever more rugged.

One day I began to climb, until at last I reached the summit, a broad, rocky plateau where a single tree grew. Breathless from climbing, I clung to the tree, and as I looked out over the water of the Sound a strange and awesome feeling came over me. I felt as if I were the only person on earth who had ever seen this sight. Woodsmoke rose from the clearing that was the town of Dasamonquepeuk. The water lapped silver against the opposite shore. And beyond—beyond stretched groves of green, gold, bronze, orange—hills and valleys, forever, forever, as far as the eye could see, as far as a man could wander in a lifetime.

The love of land was new to me, and I didn't

express it, even to myself. But I was drawn again and again to this plateau, my plateau, and I began to imagine myself a rich and free man. I would journey from here to all the strange places with their strange names—Dasamonquepeuk, Pomiock, Secota. On this plateau I would build myself a fine house; I would live here and be happy. And in my dreaming, I almost forgot about Chesapeake.

* * *

How Svenson would sputter to see me now! All in a day's work I'd help patch a roof with Master Sampson, then down to fit a window or a door, then lend a hand to Ananais with the stonecutting. And if I could do a job alone, "Go to it, then!" Ananais would say, and when it was finished he'd pause to tell me, "Well done."

Georgie Howe made himself my apprentice. For all that the others thought him dim-witted, I soon found that he anticipated my needs. I'd only begin to think of needing more nails, and there he'd be, ready with a handful. He hardly spoke, but worked along like a quiet shadow, never grumbling or complaining.

Roger Prat, in passing one day, murmured approvingly about the goodness of those who take pity on the afflicted. Georgie's expression did not change. But later he said to me, "W-W-William, do you n-need me?"

"Yes. I do need you. I want you to work with me every day."

"I will!" he exclaimed, eyes shining, but solemn

and dignified. Then I realized he'd gotten out those two words with no stutter.

It was Georgie who first approached the little children as they stood in the clearing. And when Manteo came at midday, Georgie would run to meet him. The women shook their heads and clucked their tongues, and Jane Jones even advised George Howe to keep his son close by. He thanked her sincerely and kindly, but still Georgie was allowed to wander, and at times I thought that of all of us he was the most free. He alone had a great measure of trust.

Gradually, like a nonswimmer testing the water, I became more daring myself. First a nod, then a look, then a word. Manteo liked to stand by and watch us at work. And one day I was struggling to saw off a stout limb with nobody to help, for Georgie had gone after water. Manteo watched intently for a while. Then our eyes met fully for the first time. His eyes asked the question. Mine replied. He walked toward me and grasped the other end of the saw. After one or two false starts we achieved the rhythm. The saw moved smoothly as our bodies swayed. The branch dropped, and something seemed to have been settled.

Any tool fascinated Manteo. I had to explain each one and its use. He would test it for himself, frowning in concentration, then smiling.

"It is good."

Of everything that did its work well he said, "It is good."

He showed the yeomen how to plant corn, how to take cuttings from young fruit trees, how to spread ashes over the furrows. "It is good."

In turn, he gazed at our marvels—knives, mirrors, hatchets, saws. But what interested him the most was the harquebus.

He asked me, "You have a fire stick?"

"No. They are expensive."

"Much copper."

"Yes."

"It is stronger than the arrow," he said. "I know."

"Faster, yes."

"It does not end." He made a circling motion with his hand. "The bullet—it lives in the air."

I had learned that his questions were always spoken in the same tone as statements.

"No," I said. "A bullet shoots only once, like an arrow. It shoots once. Then it ends. It dies."

"Harawok says it lives and kills again. Harawok says it brings sickness. There was sickness when Governor Lane was here. Killing with the fire stick, then the sickness."

I asked him, as we squatted down beside a shallow stream, "If you shoot an enemy with your arrow, and later your enemy's brother dies from sickness, who made him die?"

"The gods," Manteo replied.

"It's the same with us," I said.

He asked me, while he roasted fresh fish wrapped in leaves, "The white man prayed to his God, and many of our people were healed. With bullets, white men make sickness come or stay away?"

"If the white men had brought the sickness with their fire stick, then why would they take it away again?"

Confusion showed in his dark eyes. Then he told me, "With Lane came a man, Hariot. He spoke to us from the big book. He told us to sing songs. He spoke to us about his God, Jesus Christ. He said this is the God of love. In the battle I heard one man call out, 'Christ! Our victory!' Then I saw him. In his hands he was holding the head of Chief Pemisipan. Does the white God of love say it is good?"

I sat tense, silent and shivering. Heathen! How dare he question Christ's love! The name of Christ, issuing from the savage's mouth was a blasphemy. He moved one hand slightly, and I wanted to shrink back, away from his darkness, away from his possible touch which might poison me, steal the very soul out of my body. For might not the devil be brown, gleaming with sweat, yet smiling?

He did not see my fear and revulsion. Or he did not understand it.

He spoke again. "Tell me these things."

I glanced at him, saw the tremor of a muscle in his jaw, heard the quick breathing through his parted lips. The cross around my neck felt heavy and hot, as if a piercing beam of sunshine had been suddenly directed to it, and I heard again Roger Prat's admonition, "We cannot turn our faces away from them . . . you were called."

Again Manteo was murmuring about Hariot, that

wise and noble scholar who had showed him the Book. "Sing!" Manteo urged me. "Make signs! Make stories!"

Memories rushed together in my mind—the high vaulted church on Fleet Street; Dame Broody only half listening as we droned, "and thou shalt not . . ."; my mother's face shining in the candlelight as she heard my bedtime prayers, "and help us to turn away from earthly desires. . . ."

How could I tell it? Let him go to Roger Prat who was holy, or to Tom Stevens, the lawyer, whose sharp wit could make even foolish words seem wise.

"I don't know enough!" I burst out, but Manteo only nodded.

"Hariot also said this," he told me gravely.

I gazed at the bow he wore around his shoulder, at the dagger sharp arrows in his pouch. "Will you teach me your ways?" I asked.

"I will," he said. *"Ne tab.* I am your friend. *Ne tab."* And, so saying, he rose and placed his hands on my arms. For a long time afterward I still felt the touch of his hands.

* * *

Day after day soldiers searched the length and breadth of the island. The trumpet call rang out, always the same. We spoke of little else. Just a year ago fifteen Englishmen had been put ashore, with provisions to last the winter. How could fifteen men simply disappear without a trace?

* * *

The dispute raged all morning. Work was at a

standstill. The question had all the marks of one of those riddles that amuse men endlessly as they sit over their evening wine. But this was in earnest.

"It's unthinkable to build a settlement without a wall!" cried John Spendlove. "What's to protect our possessions? These flimsy houses?"

"But you see how quickly a fort can crumble," argued John Sampson. "What use is a wall, really?"

"Gentlemen," said Richard Berry stiffly, obviously restraining himself, "never in all history has any land been won and held without a certain show of force. There's absolutely no question. We must rebuild the walls of the fort."

"The women need a roof over their heads first," put in Dyonis Harvie solemnly. His wife, too, was with child. As usual, nobody listened to him.

Contemptuously Maurice Allen put in, "If you've just bought a valuable horse, what shall you build first? The fence to keep him in, or his winter stall?"

Of all of them, only Ananais leaned first toward one side of the argument, then to the other. "We must keep an open mind," he said. "The Governor feels that if we build a wall it might offend the savages."

"Offend the savages!" cried Chris Cooper, bent over with laughter. "How does one offend a savage?"

"By behaving in a way that seems rude and hostile," Ananais said gravely, and Cooper burst out laughing again.

Thoughtfully Roger Prat spoke up, rising as he

did so. "If we wish to reach them," he said, "it seems wrong to first build a wall."

"We must consider our objectives," said the lawyer, Stevens, puffing out his chest for a long-winded lecture. "We must define our purpose in coming here. Is it to bring religion to the savages? Are we willing to sacrifice ourselves for this lofty, though impractical goal? Or did we come to claim and hold this land, to establish rule over it? If *that* is the case, then our actions are prescribed by *this* goal, and our physical survival is the only valid concern. Next, we must ask ourselves, is power better won by persuasion, or by superior strength, including all the signs and symbols of such strength? . . ."

I could picture the very process of decay taking place before my eyes, while Stevens droned on eternally, each point leading to another.

"Go and fetch the Governor," Ananais whispered to me, and with relief I went to find him.

I found him near the beach, speaking to Captain Spicer. "So," I heard him say, "our men will return with you on the flyboat, and I'll prepare a letter for Raleigh requesting that *you* be in command of the supply ships."

When the Governor turned to me, I gave the message. "The Assistants ask that you decide, sir," I concluded, "whether we ought to build a wall first or finish mending the huts. And some," I added, "think we ought not to build a wall at all."

He turned to me, smiling in a half-serious, half-jesting way and asked, "What do you think, William?"

The question brought me up short, as if it were an obstacle in my path. Never before had anyone asked me what I thought.

"In truth," I stammered, "I'm not sure." His silence forced me to think about it, and we walked, all the arguments I'd heard tumbled together in my mind.

"Well, William?" he prompted, waiting for my reply.

"A wall," I began, "might make us feel safer at night. And yet, I hear the natives build no walls, and George Howe has told me how it feels to be out—out in the open spaces with only a sky for cover and no walls at all. I think," I said slowly, "if it were possible to build a town without a wall, and to live there without being afraid—it would be a fine thing. John Sampson said that the wall we build to keep them out will also keep us in. And I—I don't think I want to be kept in, sir."

He walked beside me silently, and at last I asked, with a sudden touch of fear, "Have you already made your decision, sir?"

He flashed me a stern, astonished look, then he laughed heartily. "What you mean, my young friend, is, am I asking you to make the decision?" Again he chuckled, then said, "Yes, I have made the decision, based on a different reason from yours. Though your arguments," he added quickly, "are good ones. We will not build a wall. A wall won't make us any stronger than we are. We are stronger than the savages, in many ways, but . . . it's all in the way you look at it. If we could see ourselves not as conquerors, but as guests. . . ." His voice faded, then resumed its strength. "After all, Roanoke is not to be our home. We're moving to Chesapeake next year, and until then we need the friendship of these natives. We have to move into their lives gradually, make ourselves blend into the countryside, so to speak. A wall would only teach them to fear us, and fear always turns into violence in the end."

"Do you think Wanchese is afraid of us?"

Governor White nodded. "He is very much afraid of us. Most of the other savages think we are gods. Wanchese knows we are not, and that is the source of his great fear."

We had come to the workmen, who were still disputing, and I regretted the end of our conversation. With a few well-chosen words he directed the men, and they went back to work repairing the huts and clearing roadways.

Eventually the fallen logs of Lane's old wall were hauled away or used for repairing other structures. We did erect an archway to mark the entrance to our settlement. To the post we attached a large bell, which would summon the people to meeting, to church, or as some darkly predicted, to battle.

The first time the bell called us to worship we were delighted. The rich, full sound rang out across the virgin land, announcing joyfully that we had come, and we were gathered here as a community. The sound of the bell stirred us all. "Just like home," said Mistress Viccars, and Jane Pierce added, "Look, even the savages have heard and are coming! We have brought it with us—everything, and soon other towns will rise up around us."

Roger Prat spoke glowingly of a glorious experiment, where civilized and godly men had brought the best of their traditions across the sea to begin anew.

Manteo, watching the service beside me, was moved to murmur, "It is good."

On that Sunday we all felt infused with the spirit of goodness. We moved gently and spoke softly, smiled at one another and saw the grandeur of the land through the nobility of our own feelings.

It was all shattered two days later, when the bell rang out in sudden alarm. And then it began to toll in slow, measured, mournful tones. Over and over, for hours, it continued, the death knell. Again and again, from white and rigid lips his name was spoken in disbelief and horror and anguish. George Howe was dead. George Howe had been murdered. Sixteen arrows were found in his corpse. His head had been smashed with wooden clubs.

ELEVEN

ROGER PRAT'S GRAY BEARD trembled with the violence of his feeling. Under his arm he clutched a large cross, newly fashioned from two rough boards. "They say we cannot mark George Howe's grave with the cross!" he shouted. "Are we to bury him without a sign, like an animal? Have we no shame? Have we no fear of the Lord?"

Our small community had been broken. And what should have been a day of prayer and mourning, became a day of anger and hatred turned inward, toward each other.

"But we cannot!" shouted the Governor. "The men who killed George Howe would desecrate his grave. They would mutilate his corpse—let him rest in peace," he pleaded. "Our Lord knows every one of His own. Does He need a marker? I charge you!" he said in a thundering voice, until there was silence in the small clearing, "I charge you, turn your thoughts to the soul of our friend, which has already risen to life everlasting. Will we stand here and cast lots over his poor bones, as Christ's enemies fought over his cloak? Look, instead, to his son. Take young George to your hearts and love him as godparents, one and all. Spare him this shame."

Georgie sat mute, white faced, rigid. The women wept over him, but he remained immobile. The men had tried to keep him away, but he had screamed until at last he was allowed to see his father's blood-soaked body and splintered skull. He had seen, and now he was silent.

Over Georgie's head the argument raged. "I will not conduct a pagan burial!"

The Governor stood beside the open grave, saying, "Let us pray."

But Roger Prat would not be moved. He planted the cross between two rocks and remained there on his knees, with several of his followers behind him. When it was over, and the hymn was sung, we walked in procession down the hill, but Roger Prat still remained on his knees.

Near dusk he came down, carrying the cross. His teeth were set against pain. He had removed his shoes to let the sharp stones cut and wound his feet as he walked.

Still the argument raged, hotter now that night was approaching. Richard Berry had laid battle plans for revenge. This, he shouted, was the moment, and it must be met.

Christopher Cooper headed the list of volunteers. Beyond words now, they made the age-old preparations for combat.

With intricate logic, lawyer Stevens spoke for a show of power. Unless we proved our ability to answer attack for attack, he said, we were doomed.

And again, Ananais Dare hung between, turning his ear first to one side, then the other. Dyonis Harvie murmured halfheartedly about forbearance; we had women and children to consider. And John Sampson put the question most simply: upon whom were we to revenge ourselves? Who had murdered George Howe?

"Who else but Wanchese?" cried Cooper, flushed and eager.

"And even if it wasn't Wanchese," shouted Berry, "the savages must learn to keep their own kind in hand."

Governor White had listened to them all in turn. Now he ordered silence. "There will be no battle," he said, lifting both hands in the gesture of power. "We have made mistakes before—I have been here, and I know. We have done butchery before, and the need for vengeance is satisfied only for the moment. The scars linger. I have talked at length to Manteo. He tells me that the natives of Roanoke are innocent. He invites us to travel to Croatoan, to meet with the chiefs, to form an alliance. The Croatoans have always been friendly to us. They fear the murdering bands as much as we do, for they are peaceful people. In two days' time we will go to Croatoan for counsel—I and others whom I will choose."

* * *

"*Ne tab*," said Manteo, when I asked the reason for the dark painted lines on his face. "*Ne tab*," he said to Georgie, as he flung specks of powder into the fire, then sat down in the posture of sorrow. "Your friend and father is dead, and I mourn for him with you."

Manteo picked up a stout branch. With a lighted torch he proceeded to burn out its center, speaking softly all the while to Georgie, explaining that this was how canoes were fashioned. "It moves lightly and swiftly, like the souls of the dead," he said. "For our friends we make such a ship, when they are dead, that it can be laid beside them. In it the soul moves to—to . . ."

"H-heaven," said Georgie.

Manteo nodded. "Yes, it is the word Hariot taught me. Maybe your Book does not tell about the ship. But I think this Heaven is the same place we know. Your God will not be angry if you take this ship from a friend."

Slowly Georgie limped toward Manteo, stretched out his hand, then looked at me questioningly.

"It's a fine gift," I said, and my throat tightened. "Take it, Georgie."

Gravely Georgie took the small canoe, and the three of us sat together in silence.

At last I had to ask, "Do you know who killed him, Manteo?"

"I do not."

"Was it Wanchese?"

"I do not know."

"Have you seen him? Does he know we have landed?"

"I have not seen him. I think he knows." Manteo's face became passive, expressionless.

"He was your friend, wasn't he," I stated.

"Yes." He sighed, stood up to flick a last bit of powder into the ashes. The fire flared briefly, then died down. "It is all gone," he said, and I knew he meant not only the fire. "He was my friend. More, my brother, and even more. Wanchese and I were together on Wokokon the day the first ships came; the white-skinned ones walked beside us even before they went to the priests or the chiefs."

"And they took you both," I murmured, "to England."

"Yes. It was an honor that we were chosen. My people thought they were gods."

Of course—what else could they have thought? The sails of our explorers' ships seemed to them like wings. And their clothes! No earthly animal has skin so soft and brilliantly colored. How very pure and pale the Englishmen must have looked to the dark-skinned natives, and the gifts they brought seemed not to be of this earth . . . knives, hatchets, and above all the fire stick. They had no women! Who but a god could live without women?

"In the palace," Manteo continued, "with the great *Weroanca*, Elizabeth, we learned the truth. We saw how white men spin the cloth for their clothes, how they take metal and bend it into shape with fire. We saw small ones and women, and we saw that some died. And Wanchese was very angry."

"But you were not angry!" I exclaimed. "You didn't feel tricked or cheated. Does Wanchese only befriend gods?"

"I do not know Wanchese anymore," Manteo said, and his face was set against old feelings and memories. "Even when we were young, Wanchese always played the warrior. It is his way."

* * *

Hugh came running to me, shouting. "William! We're on the list—both of us. We're going to Croatoan!"

"We!" I exclaimed, breathless with excitement.

"The Governor wants you," Hugh replied, grinning. "Oh, it will be a fine adventure! I suppose it's because of Manteo. The Governor's seen you two together, and I think Manteo's taken a liking to you. Maybe Manteo especially asked for you."

All afternoon I wondered why I had been chosen, and as word got around many sought me out. "It's because of your fair hair," declared Maurice Allen. "Don't you see? The savages will stare at you and forget their arrows."

Roger Prat thought a different reason. It was expressed only in his eyes, in his hand on my shoulder as he murmured, "Go with God, William."

Emme Merrimoth hustled from one to the other of us, with instructions to seek out a certain mulberry tree on Croatoan. "Bring me a cutting," she pleaded, "and take it carefully. You'll know the leaf by its bright color and many points. It may be the most important thing you'll find!" she warned.

Jane Pierce ran toward me with a request of her own. "William," she coaxed breathlessly, large eyes gleaming, "you'll want a new pair of breeches for winter, and I shall make them for you myself. Only find me a fine token from Croatoan."

"What token, Mistress Pierce?" I asked, puzzled. "Croatoan is only a native village, not an English town."

"A bit of weaving or pottery," she replied, "or some small jewel. The natives use them as trinkets—pearls and sometimes even gold. A large medallion of beaten copper would do. I've quite a collection gathered already," she said with pride, and I was astounded. Somehow she had already established a commerce with the savages. I wondered what treasures lay in her trunks now, and what she might do with them.

"I'll try," I told her.

"You must! What's the use of traveling unless one brings back something new?"

When Elizabeth heard I was going to Croatoan, her face took on a dark expression. "Why do you have to go? There's still so much to do here."

"I *want* to go," I snapped. "I didn't come all this way just to sit in one spot."

She looked at me coldly. "You're not a soldier."

"We don't want soldiers this time," I replied. "There will be only twenty of us, and the Governor has chosen *me*. The soldiers will stay here to protect you," I teased, "so you won't need me at all."

"I don't need you anyway," she retorted. "Mistress Dare has asked me to stay in her house. You don't have to be responsible for me anymore, William. I'm to live in her house and help her—when the baby comes." She blushed.

"I'll be glad to see you doing women's work," I muttered, and she smiled up at me and smoothed her hair.

"I'm doing everything!" she exclaimed proudly. "Old Agnes Wood is no use at all. Mistress Dare says she hardly knows what she'd do without me. Mistress Dare says I'll make some man a good wife." Her face grew redder still. Then quickly she said, "Remember, Mistress Dare wants you to make her a cradle. We're already making little clothes."

"The cradle will be ready in time," I said. "I've already chosen a fine piece of cedar for it."

That evening as I sat by the fire I began to carve out the front panel for the cradle. Manteo came to sit beside me. Presently he asked, "The girl you call Elizabeth is your sister?"

"No. I look after her."

"Like a brother."

"I suppose so," I said. "At least for now. She is nearly—a woman." Having said this I realized it was true. Lately she had taken to wearing dresses, and often I heard her talking to the other women about cooking and stitchery.

"You do not court her," Manteo stated.

"No. She is—she is not—I only look after her."

Manteo nodded soberly. "I also have a little sister like that. She is the child of my mother's sister. On Croatoan you will see her. Telana. I have told her about white men. Her eyes will open in wonder at your yellow hair," he said, laughing. "I have told her of men with yellow hair and eyes like the sky. She only laughs. I think she does not believe it. And strange, because her skin is light. She is a child of the legend."

"Her skin . . ."

"Not light as yours, not dark as mine. She is a child of the legend," he repeated.

He told me the legend, and as it unfolded I felt as if a door were opening before me. Long afterward my mind would return to this moment and this legend:

"It happened many seasons before I was born, on the Island of Wokokon. Wokokon, the holy place, where no man lives, but many go to seek visions. In this long time of seasons before I was born, men from Secota came to Wokokon to gather wild grapes and hunt the white birds. That day no clouds were in the sky. Yet when they looked out to sea they saw great white mysteries, like clouds, like white wings. The white wings came closer. Then the men of Secota saw that they carried a large canoe. Secota men fell down on the sand to pray. Then white-skinned beings came down from the winged ship and walked on the sand. Hair curled and waved on their faces! Their bodies shone and gleamed.

They spoke a strange, heavenly tongue, these white gods from beyond the land of the sea and the sky.

"Secota men took the white gods to their town. Harawok, the priest, a young man then, welcomed them. Harawok gave them many prayers and offerings. All belonged to them. All was for their use. Then the white gods made new wings for their ships, using the white stuff of their garments. Under the wings they sailed away to the land of the sea and the sky.

"When gods appear they leave gifts. So it was. Many days later the Secota found the gifts. The canoe of the white gods lay empty on the beach. The white gods had disappeared. The priests said that they no longer needed their ship. Their wings had carried them back to the sky. But buried in the wood of the flying ship the Secota found the gifts, sharp spikes stronger than rock. From these the Secota made their best weapons. And not only these, but they left us a sign. After a time three women of Secota bore children. Their skin was pale. Not as pale as the pure whiteness of the gods, but nearly so. The gods do not give everything of themselves, but only a part, so we may remember and honor them."

Manteo said all this in the singsong tone of a storyteller who repeats ancient lore word for word. Then, though his face wore the rigid, impassive mask, he sighed and said, "It is hard for me. Harawok still teaches the legend, and most of our people . . ." he made a vague, helpless gesture.

"But Telana," I prompted. "You said she is a child of the legend."

"After a time," he repeated, "three women of Secota bore children. Their skin was pale. Telana's mother was one of these children. The sign is given to Telana through her."

"But when you told Telana about the white men who are not gods . . ." I began.

"It does not matter," he replied. "Telana is loved, and she would be loved even without the sign. She laughs and sings. You will see. And she wants to know everything! 'Make stories,' she says, 'Tell me wonders!' All winter I stayed on Croatoan with her and my mother. I have tried to teach her your language. It is a game for her. You will see. You will like my little sister."

*   *   *

It was the night before our journey to Croatoan. I had put out the last fire, and in the scant moonlight I thought it was a vision, that softly moving shape, the faintly whispered calling, the hair like silver in the moonlight. Margaret Lawrence moved toward me, her skirts rustling, and rapidly, like the fluttering of a bird she whispered. I was overwhelmed by her nearness, so that I couldn't speak. She whispered on about gold and pearls and Chesapeake, whispered strange rumors while her hands touched my face. "They say the Governor plans secretly to go to Chesapeake, that he is impatient to find the treasure. It is all false, this visit to Croatoan, and you shall be among the first to see the river of pearls."

Her fingertips lay against my cheek, and the warm, strong scent of lavender mingled with whirling flashes of thought about legends of gods and treasures, jewel mines that glittered, rivers of pearls.

"I shall watch your possessions for you while you are gone," she whispered, and for a moment I awakened.

"What possessions? I own nothing."

"Your possessions," she murmured, and her fingertips soothed me.

I felt stupid and drugged, and my words were thick and meaningless. Something, it seemed, had been promised, in exchange for a few stolen kisses, and then she was gone.

* * *

Manteo and I stood at the bow of the pinnace as we sailed due south toward Croatoan. Around his neck he wore the trinkets we had given him, *rupees*, he called them. His cheeks were smooth and glistened with oil. Early that morning he had plucked out the few hairs from his chin, and on each cheek he had painted a white, upward stroke, like lines of laughter.

"It is good to be going home," I remarked, and he smiled. I asked, "Will your father be there to meet us?"

"My father lives at Chawanook where he is chief."

"And you will be chief someday?"

"No. Chiefs are born only from noble women.

When I was very small my mother took me away to live at Croatoan. It is our law. My father must take other wives to bear him more sons. He is very wise, my father," Manteo added quickly. "He commands 700 warriors. He travels far to meet with other chiefs. But it is hard for him. He is lame."

"I'd like to see your father."

"The time will come," Manteo said calmly, and even as we neared Croatoan, his face showed no emotion.

We went down from the ship, and Manteo prepared to lead the way. How must he feel, I wondered, to be coming home—to know every rise and fall of the land, every tree, every face.

The Governor motioned him to wait. "You and I," he said, "will walk together."

Manteo glanced at the Governor's harquebus. "You take the fire stick?"

"We must," the Governor replied. "But we hope not to use our weapons. Tell them we are coming in peace."

"Not one arrow will leave the bow," Manteo promised. We set out slowly from the beach, and Manteo cupped his hand to his mouth, calling out in greeting.

But no answer came from the hills, and Hugh muttered, "Where are they all? I don't like this silence."

"Maybe the men went off hunting," I said, but the strange desolation sent a chill over me. A bird called shrilly. The sound faded to a soft clucking. Then even the birds were silent.

Leaving the beach behind us, we came to the mouth of a gorge, overgrown with dry and tangled shrubs. Again Manteo called. His cry resounded from the sides of the canyon, bringing us eerie echoes upon echoes. Scarcely had the last echo faded, than a new sound came ringing from above. It was the growling, howling sound that wild things make, the terror-filling sound that everyone knows in his nightmares and recognizes at once as the sound of danger, the cry of attack.

Above us, like images carved from stone, stood some forty warriors, poised as one, bowstrings taut, arrows pointed downward. As one, we saw them, and for a long, hideous instant time froze.

Then came the flashing and clatter of swords swiftly drawn, and guns being readied for firing. Run-fight-run-fight . . . inside came the great, hot surging, and I clutched my knife, heard a dull, fierce throbbing in my head. Drums, I thought with that last spark of reason, drums and death, drums and death go together.

TWELVE

THE DRUMS—THE DRUMS were in my head and nowhere else. The battle that was beating inside my head never even began, for in the next moment bows and arrows were flung to the ground, and Manteo was caught in the embrace of his kinsmen.

"They did not know me," Manteo explained; and I wondered, can't they even tell each other apart? Are they really no different from bitches and hounds who forget even how to recognize their own young?

"They are very afraid of wild bands who rob their grain," Manteo continued. "They guard the village." He turned to his countrymen, then to the Governor. "I told them we come for counsel, that you will not harm their crop. It has been a bad year, and they have only a little."

Suddenly two savages grasped my arms, their joy

at seeing Manteo had overflowed to the rest of us. They pumped my hands, touched me all over, until Manteo called out sharply to stop them.

"The headman says now we have feast," Manteo explained.

"Tell him," said Governor White, "we don't want to diminish their meager store of food."

"You must," Manteo said firmly. "It is for friendship."

Governor White bowed slightly. "Tell them we are honored."

We were led by the natives to their village. On the path they paused to point to an old man, limping from a wounded leg that would not heal.

Manteo explained, "He was shot by Lane's company. They mistook him for one of Pemisipan's warriors. My friends say they know it was a mistake. They do not blame you. But they beg for a token, a strip of white cloth to bind to their arms. Then you would know them from the others and never shoot them."

Beads of bone, copper and pearls adorned the chiefs who waited outside their huts. Manteo spoke to them briefly. Solemnly they embraced our Governor and motioned him inside.

"Manteo, I'll need you," said Governor White, looking perplexed as a schoolboy. "How can I speak to the chiefs without you?"

"Conference is for tomorrow," Manteo told him. "Now you eat. I cannot eat with chiefs." He smiled. "Do not worry, they give you much to eat."

Hugh, being led away by four clamoring savages, grinned at me in passing. Several grasped me by the arms, but Manteo sent them sternly away. I was to go with him, he said, and my relief was great. The eyes of the other savages were too eager or too veiled, and their flesh gave off a strong, heavy odor.

Little boys stared at us as we made our way to Manteo's hut. Squaws put their hands to their mouths. An old, old woman knelt as we passed and put out her hand to touch my footprint in the dust.

On a slight knoll we stopped to look down at the cluster of huts with their gently rounded roofs. "There is my mother's house," Manteo said, pointing. We passed between the trees. Then Manteo said softly, "Telana."

She was sitting outside the hut, bent over a large stone bowl. At first, as she swayed, bringing the pestle down against the grain, I could not see her face. In the filtered sun her black hair shone as if it were wet, moving gently along her back. The rhythm of her body was like a dance, broken suddenly by Manteo's call, "Telana!"

She sprang up and ran toward him, while I waited behind a large sassafras shrub, watching as she embraced Manteo. For the first time I noted a particular face among the many faces of savage women, and this face was somehow less tamed than those of the others, yet in another way more finely drawn. Was it her mouth, full and mobile with laughter—her wide jaw and high-set cheekbones—her slim, flashing legs, or only the color of her skin, pale bronze like flowing honey, that set her so vividly apart?

Strangely, too, her body was not exposed. She was dressed in soft deerskin from her shoulders to her knees.

She saw me and stopped short. Her expression was like that of the boldest native children, astonished, awed, yet curious. Manteo, seeing her wonder, laughed aloud. He spoke to her, and she gazed at me, then quickly lowered her eyes.

"Telana says welcome," Manteo said. In the soft tones of a crooning bird Telana murmured to him, then stood in silence looking at me as if I were a vision.

"She cannot believe that there is a real man with hair like the sun, and you are so beautiful!"

Still she gazed at me, and I don't know what my face revealed, but suddenly Manteo spoke sharply and motioned her away. "I know how you feel," Manteo said. "In your country I sat beside your *Weroanca*, Elizabeth, and white men came to look at me with eyes burning."

"It isn't that," I said. To myself I wondered, half in disgust, what is it then? Had I become so vain as to bask in the admiration of a young female savage? But savages do not look that way, my mind countered, savages are—they are not. . . ."

"Her clothing is different," I began. "Do all the Secota women dress as she does?"

"No. I told you, Telana is like your sister Elizabeth Glane. She finds her own way." He grinned. "I told her the way of white women who cover themselves. She wanted to try it. Now in late afternoon when the wind is cool she does cover herself. She told me she was glad today for her cloak, that it would please you."

"Then tell her," I said unsteadily, "that I am pleased."

Manteo's mother waited for us to approach the hut. Then she moved toward her son, mouth wide open to show large teeth gleaming like round pearls. Her face was round as a melon, and she had a body to match. Her bare breasts bobbed over the fringe of the apron she wore at her waist. Fine fat woman, the natives say, for fat women give warmth in winter.

Somehow she didn't seem surprised to see me. She nodded to me, then began persistently to question Manteo. Patiently he listened, then answered her at length.

"My mother asks, where did I find you, and was your father a chief? She asks about your age, and she says," he paused, "she says you must stay out of the sun and eat better."

I kept my face sober, as I had learned from watching Manteo, and I thanked her. She hurried away to tend an assortment of pots and bowls that steamed over the fire.

Manteo and I sat down on a long mat beside the outer wall of the hut. Overhead hung a matted canopy held up by long poles. At night or in bad weather the poles would be removed; the matting would serve as a wall.

Telana brought a flat wooden bowl filled with roasted nuts and set it down between us. She murmured something to Manteo, her eyes filled with mischief. He whispered back to her, nodding, and she said, "Eat, William Wythers." Then she hurried away to watch us from a distance.

"Won't Telana eat with us?" I asked.

"The women eat later," he said. "A woman eats with a man only when they are married, or betrothed. Even a grown son does not sit down to eat with his mother."

One after the other, Telana brought many dishes; boiled peas mixed with corn, sweet chunks of melon, small corn cakes, and a delicious combination of fruit, meat and fish all cooked together in a large pot.

I tried to follow Manteo's example, to eat only a little of each. But I'm afraid I was something of a glutton. When the mat was cleared and Telana brought a large plate of wild grapes, I could only shake my head and groan. This sent her into peals of laughter and a flutter of words. I insisted that Manteo translate. At last he told me, "Telana says that you eat like a bear before winter—a young bear who has never tasted honey before."

She had scurried to the far edge of the hut, looking angry at Manteo, afraid I would take offense.

I felt the flush on my face. "Tell her that if she will cook for me tomorrow, I will eat like a man, sensibly. I have never tasted any food so good."

I saw her smile. "She understands," Manteo said. "Now she is too strange to talk. Wait until she begins. She talks too much. You will have to send her away."

"I won't send her away," I said softly. One could as easily send away a blue jay. I watched her, wondering—child or woman? wild or tame? What kind of a man had the white-skinned grandfather been? Where was his home? Had he loved the role of white god?

"How old is Telana?" I asked.

"Fifteen."

"And still not married?"

"Many young braves have wanted her." He made a motion, like water tumbling over rocks. "She slips away from them."

Now Manteo brought out a pipe. He sucked at it, held in the vapor, then let it out in a thick cloud. He offered it to me.

"The pipe is for friendship," he said, "and good after eating. Your wise Hariot praised our *uppowok* very much. He took it back to the *Weroanca* Elizabeth, and she also took great pleasure in it."

I pulled at the pipe, coughing as smoke filled my mouth and throat. "I've heard it's good for the body humors," I said, still choking. "I'll have to get used to it."

Luckily, he didn't return the pipe again, but stood up, saying, "Now, we dance."

"We dance?" I echoed, scarcely able to budge.

"All night," Manteo replied, beaming.

Hugh was in his glory. "What a welcome they gave me!" he exclaimed when we met at the ceremonial ground. "They washed my feet, they combed my beard. These native women know how to give hospitality!"

He nodded toward the center of the ceremonial circle, where Telana stood with two other girls. "That one's well favored," he murmured. "I wouldn't mind . . ."

"She's Manteo's cousin," I said quickly, reluctant, somehow, to tell him more.

From behind the trees came the sudden clatter of rattles, a ringing and joyful shouting. A dozen young braves, their bodies boldly painted, ran to the ceremonial circle. Each took his place beside a tall post. Faces were carved into these posts, faces that strangely resembled coifed nuns, their expressions prayerful and mild.

Wild and frenzied was the dancing that now began. The braves twisted and turned in fantastic postures. They chanted and roared, shook their rattles, clapped their hands. They leaped and kicked and pranced, while in the center the three girls gently swayed and turned.

My muscles tensed at their movements. The drumming, the singing, the pattern of the dance worked itself into my senses, bearing down until I saw and heard and felt nothing else. Up came the rattles, then a shake, shake, shaking, down the dark hands, clapping together, then rush to the center and back. Faster and faster, the rhythm demanded that dancers respond—faster and faster, till one of the braves leaped away from the circle and another jumped into his place.

My feet twitched with an inner tapping. Hugh beat his fist against his palm. The singing grew louder, more jubilant, the beat more insistent. With a sudden leap Hugh sprang into the circle of dancers. A cheer arose from the natives, the tempo quickened, and Hugh in his red satin breeches and flying blue cloak danced with complete abandon.

Something or someone seemed to pull me— Telana's eyes, half-closed and heavy lidded, seemed to draw me up. Someone pressed a gourd into my hand. One leap, and I found myself in their very midst, *dancing!* Oh, I cannot tell you how it's done, and I had never danced before. Are we all born knowing how to dance? And do we only wait to hear the right music? That night I got the right music. Dancing, I was somehow bound to the earth and all the people on it, yet also soaring, soaring with eagles . . .

We danced until the huge logs were burned into coals. Then we sank down and slept under the trees.

* * *

"William Wythers!" she said. "Come."

She would show me the island, Manteo said, while the chiefs held counsel with the Governor and our three Assistants, and the rest of us were free to explore.

"William Wythers!" Telana smiled at the sound

of the new words, and I followed after her. We walked through the village of huts, past the vegetable plots and the ceremonial circle, and she said not a word. At last we came to a hut without walls, a thatched roof supported by poles, where at eye level was a platform, and under it sat a priest tending a low fire. Upon the platform lay a row of skeletons, neatly and closely placed. It was the burial house, and these were the remains of honored chiefs.

I bore the shocking sight without the flicker of an eye. She rewarded me with the words, "Good you come here, William Wythers," and with a smile.

She took me to the fields where tall cornstalks grew. "*Pagotowr*," she told me. Between the stalks they had planted beans. "*Okindgier*," Telana said, picking a long bean for me to taste.

"Bean," I said.

"Bean," she repeated, laughing. We made a game of it.

"*Macoquer!*"

"Melon."

"*Wichonzowr!*"

"Peas."

She ran, laughing, from one crop to the next. Finally she sat down at the edge of the cornfield, plucked out a kernel and held it in her palm.

"From this come cakes," she told me. In a mixture of words and gestures she gave me to understand that the kernel could also be roasted in oil until it grew large and white. "Makes noise like fire stick far away," she said, with a clap of her hands.

"A bang," I supplied. Putting my finger in my mouth, I created a loud popping sound. I had learned this as a child, much to my mother's annoyance.

"Yes!" she cried, very pleased. "I cook this for you tonight."

We moved to the silent ceremonial ground and sat down on a log. After several minutes she asked me hesitantly, "Are you a *Weroance*?"

"A chief?" I had to laugh. "No."

"But this—hair—like the sun. Manteo speaks of great *Weroanca* with hair like the sun going down, red."

I shook my head, bewildered.

"Manteo speaks of a man, *Ralee*. Wear so fine clothes. Manteo says *Ralee* has hair like sun—too. He is a *Weroance*, yes."

I nodded. "Yes, I suppose you could say that Walter Raleigh is a chief." Now I understood her problem, and I told her, "It is not the color of the hair that makes a *Weroance*, a chief."

"It is not color."

"No."

"*Ayee*," she sighed. "It is good."

She held out her hand, asking the question with her eyes. I let her touch my hair.

"Manteo says the great *Weroanca* has no man," she told me earnestly. "Why is it?"

I kept my face equally sober, though inside I was bursting with laughter. I had heard this question argued endlessly in the pubs and streets and villages of England. Now, here it was again!

"I do not know," I confessed.

"Do you have a woman?"

I was startled. "No."

"Why not?"

I shrugged, while my mind flashed over the women of our company: the widow Pierce with her fluttering, gathering hands; Elizabeth, pesky and demanding as a puppy; and Margaret, Margaret Lawrence. Suddenly my face burned at the remembrance of those stolen kisses, and the fire they had aroused in me.

"We have a problem," I said, half teasing. She didn't understand.

"Make courtship gift," she suggested. "Your father choose fine fat woman for you."

"My father is dead," I told her. "And my mother, too."

"*Ayee!*" she cried in deep sympathy. "You are alone!"

"No, I have friends." I looked at her fully, felt a strange sense of peace together with a mad beating. "Will you be my friend too?"

"*Ne tab* . . . I am your friend. We are the same. I tell you. My mother, my father are dead. It was the Pomiock. The Pomiock and my people, Secota, had peace. It was good."

And she told me this tale of treachery. The Pomiock and the Secota were at peace, having forgiven their differences. One day the Pomiock invited the Secota to a great feast. They went, many of the chiefs, the warriors, the women. But Telana was very small, and she was left with her father's sister. While the Secota were feasting and praying, the Pomiock warriors attacked them with arrows and clubs, killing nearly all of them.

She told this in the calm, patient way of the storyteller, but then she grasped my arm for a brief moment and said fiercely, "Never go to Pomiock!"

I asked Telana how long ago this had happened, and she was puzzled. "Time," I prompted. "How much time ago?"

She shook her head and said simply, "Long, long away back. It does not matter."

I began to have some inkling, then, that my notion of time was completely unknown to her. In the next months I would learn that time, in the Indian way, is an endless thread. They do not count the minutes or hours as we do. The fact that the sun rises and sets, that season follows season in orderly course, is simply accepted as part of the whole way. They live within this ebb and flow of time, never struggling against it or regretting that they must grow old. Time is like a river, and they flow with it.

Telana stood up and took my hand. "Come," she said. "I thank the gods that you are here."

She led me down a narrow path through the trees to a small hut, built like the others, but without a door. Inside on a raised platform sat an idol made of wood. It sat cross-legged, like a man; it was dressed like a man in an apron of deerskin, its neck adorned with beads of copper. But the face was horrible, slashed into a menacing grimace.

Telana stood silently before the idol. "He would not know me," she murmured. Quickly she slipped the cloak from her shoulders and fastened it again at her waist.

At the sight of her standing thus, my breath caught in my throat. I gazed at her, and unashamed, for what I felt was not the hot, tormenting lust I'd known before. But I was filled with a gentle warmth, born of surprise and new awareness, as when I had found my secret plateau and thought, yes, here it is.

When she had finished praying and pulled up her cloak once more, she said gaily, "Come! I cook for you now."

As we walked back to the village, she told me about her many gods, about a heaven called *Mohomny*, and a black pit called *Popogusso* where the wicked go after death. I told her about the one God.

"Only one!" she exclaimed, disappointed.

"One," I said firmly. "Our God doesn't want us to pray to others. I could not pray to your god," I said with a wave toward the shrine.

"No matter." She smiled. "I have prayed to *Kewas* for you."

* * *

From the Croatoan chiefs Governor White learned that it was Wanchese and his band who had killed George Howe. Croatoan scouts had watched the Wingos land on Roanoke. They had seen the Wingos stalking among the reeds by the stream where George Howe stood hunting for crabs. I wondered, had they watched the murder? Yes, they had simply watched—hollow men, they had watched my friend murdered and done nothing. As to Grenville's men—this too they had described to the Governor. The Wingos had lured the Englishmen out of their huts, pretending friendship. They set fire to the huts, and as the men ran away the Wingos pursued them with clubs and arrows, until every one of the fifteen lay dead.

I was filled with loathing. And yet, on the way back to Roanoke, Governor White told us, "We will forget the past. In seven days there will be a meeting on Roanoke. The Croatoan will come to us for talks, and meanwhile they will gather all the other chiefs of all the other tribes who want peace."

Well then, the Governor was better at forgiveness than I! As we sat in the pinnace with Croatoan behind us, I felt as if a spell had been cast over me for the last two days. I had forgotten everything else in my pleasure. The face of a young savage girl had made me forget that the natives were hollow. I had been glad that Telana was coming with us to Roanoke. I had gazed at her beautiful face only with pleasure that she had chosen to come to see the colonists. Now I realized that even their spirits were horrors, like those bones in the burial hut and the hideous *Kewas* in the shrine. Yes, they could play like children, and they played at innocence. But something was missing in them that they could not know right from evil. To watch murder and treachery—to tell it with passive faces—I could not hold them innocent.

THIRTEEN

AGAIN, THE ARGUMENTS, the cries for vengeance, the pleading for restraint. We would wait seven days for the natives to accept our offer of peace, to come to Roanoke for counsel. Those who did not come would thereby show themselves as our enemies. The offer of peace extended to all the tribes, even to Wanchese and the Wingos.

For seven days we waited. No one came. And at midnight of the seventh day we moved out to battle against Wanchese.

The soldiers who had marched out so gladly at midnight, returned the next noon, straggling, weary, and ashamed.

Yes, they had caught the savages by complete surprise. Manteo had led them across the Sound to Dasamonquepeuk, then north to where the Wingos had last been seen. Our men had spotted the fires from an encampment, then circled around to cut off every escape. "Christ our victory!" came the battle call, and then the rout as the terrified savages fled under the roar of guns. One had been wounded and another killed before our soldiers heard the rasping voice in the darkness.

"Cap'n! Friend! We Croatoan!"

The Croatoan had come to gather the crops left behind by the fleeing Wingos. Their scouts had seen the Wingos leaving.

"They needed food," Manteo explained.

"But why didn't they come to us?" we cried. "We said seven days—we thought. . . ."

"They needed food," he repeated. "Later, talk."

Our soldiers had helped the Croatoan gather up the abandoned grain, tobacco and squash. The Croatoan bore their dead warrior away on a litter, and they begged for a sign, a bit of white cloth. Said one of the Croatoan chiefs, "We look all same to you," and the Governor promised that white cloth would be given.

Among the Croatoan was the wife of Menantenon, carrying a baby on her back. The young wife, Quinsha, was half dead from fright. Our soldiers had brought her and the baby in our pinnace to Roanoke.

"It was their own fault," Hugh told me, when the battle was recounted again. "Even Manteo says it would never have happened if they'd come to us as they'd promised. Lord, we might have slaughtered them all! Well, I suppose they've learned that the white man's word is as good as his deeds."

I shivered and swallowed down an outraged reply, but it went down hard.

* * *

The next Sunday, in recognition of his faithful service, Manteo was christened.

"By the power granted to me as Governor of Virginia, by command of Sir Walter Raleigh and in the name of her Majesty, Queen Elizabeth of England, I christen thee, Manteo, Lord of Roanoke and Dasamonquepeuk."

Manteo knelt, wearing a new cloak of pale deerskin and a brilliant headdress of white and scarlet feathers. The natives of Roanoke sat cross-legged on the ground, staring mutely while Roger Prat told his sermon: "So the heathen shall come to fear the name of the Lord!"

We sang, and the savages raised their hands. They swayed to the tune; their faces shone, eyes came alive.

When it was over Manteo and Telana asked me whether they might touch the Book. I took them to Roger Prat. He let them touch the Bible and press it to their lips.

To the watching colonists Prat called, "You see how they hunger after the true God!"

"It seems to me," Maurice Allen cackled, "the savage wench hungers for our light-haired friend!"

Richard Berry turned on him in a rage. "I'm sure William finds your words disgusting, as I do."

Chris Cooper, his face washed in sweat, nudged

the man beside him, whispered something, and they laughed.

Suddenly I saw the widow Pierce reach out her hand and take the edge of Telana's cloak between her fingers. "Fine fur," she murmured. "Would you like to make a trade?"

"No!" The word burst from my lips, even before I knew what I meant by it. No to Telana—no to all of them, Allen, Berry and Prat—or did I mean no to myself?

"She does not understand," I said quickly. They all stared at me with strange wonder in their eyes.

* * *

I sat back against a tree trunk, watching the preparations for the christening feast. Men broke open fresh kegs of ale. In makeshift ovens the women baked sugar cakes and fruit breads.

I could remember Bessie's christening, and I was overcome with homesickness. Then, as now, the women had rushed about in a frenzy over their countless chores, while the men laughed louder and drank more than usual.

Even Elizabeth was fully caught up in the preparations. "Keep your fingers out of the cakes, William! They're for later."

The very same words now as then . . . and it struck me that on Croatoan I had seen the brown-skinned children dipping into the pots, and their mothers only stood back to let them eat.

"The cakes! The cakes are burned!"

"The savages won't know the difference."

"Ambrose Viccars! Put on your shoes and stockings. Just because we live among the savages is no reason to . . ."

"Bobby, your collar's filthy."

"Between watching the children and the savages . . . I caught one dipping into my store of herbs, bold as you please. Didn't even know he was there—they have a way of creeping. . . ."

"I always know when they're about. I say, you can smell them before you see them."

My shirt was soaked with sweat, and I turned away from our huts toward a sheltered pool I had found. A few days before Mistress Jones had spotted me on my return, dripping, and said, "You must beware of bathing overmuch, William. It is bad for the humors and drying to the skin."

Without thinking I'd responded, "The natives bathe every day, and their skin is smooth."

Shocked, she retorted, "Would you compare their leather skin to yours? And fish do daily bathe," she said scornfully, "but do not call themselves men!"

Now I lay back in the cool water, with the spicy fresh fragrance of leaves all around me. And as the water held me, lapping at my hair, my mind lazily formed the words, "It is good."

Refreshed for the feast, I watched the natives bringing their offerings of turkeys and fish and vegetables. Somehow a circle of colonists had formed around the three large fire pits, a circle in which there was no room for more. The colonists handed the food outward to where the natives squatted on their mats, waiting.

I brought a sugar cake to Manteo, another to Telana, and I watched her taste the new food and lick her lips. I watched her when the singing began. The recorder and the lute played in perfect harmony, like two human voices blending together. It was dark now, and from the darkness a voice came singing,

> *"Alas, my love, you do me wrong*
> *To cast me off discourteously. . . ."*

What voice was this? I strained forward to listen.

> *"And I have loved you*
> *Oh, so long. . . ."*

Elizabeth! Wantonly swaying she sang from deep in her throat, making every man look at her. Elizabeth! Were she Bessie, I would beat her. As it was I could only clench my fists—and from across the fire, as if they saw my anger, Margaret Lawrence and the widow Pierce stood whispering and laughing, and I formed vile words to call them all.

Beside me Hugh chuckled. "Some change has come over your girl. I think even old Clement's bewitched."

And indeed, when the song ended, Clement groped his way toward Elizabeth to claim her for the dance. No woman was left on the side. Sober Jane Jones stepped proudly beside her husband. Joyce Archard, at first coy and reluctant, took her husband's arm at last, while Margaret Lawrence and Christopher Cooper were paired, the widow Pierce was caught in a rapid whirl of changing partners, and even Emme Merrimoth danced.

They moved from partner to partner, as was fitting, but Elizabeth and Clement did not break apart.

"Your sister dances well," Telana said softly.

"She is not my sister!"

I took Telana's arm and brought her into the circle of dancers.

Telana rebuked me gently. "Is this your dance of war?"

I slowed my movements, glancing about for Elizabeth. Well, I was *not* responsible for her! Let her become what she wished! But I had said I would look after her . . . later, I promised myself, I would have words with her.

Gradually more and more of our men, bolder from drink and dancing, moved out to take partners from among the native women. The pattern of the dance began to change as the Indian women tried to match the now exaggerated steps and boisterous movements of the white men.

Something changed in the atmosphere. The lute missed a beat or two. The recorder went sour, struggled with a high note, then fell silent.

Mistress Viccars pressed a hand to her forehead. "I have a headache," she said, leading her husband away.

Margaret Lawrence grasped Chris Cooper's arm and pulled him aside. Then the widow Pierce said loudly, "I do not dance with savages!"

Something froze inside me, and I felt Telana stiffen, too.

"I go," she said.

* * *

In the river swam a great fish, its scales flashing green and silver. It swam upstream, between cool fronds and bending willows, following a gold, shimmering light on the water. The riverbank was laden with jewels and pearls. The fish swam easily, tirelessly, toward the golden flecks that appeared always just ahead.

A dark shadow fell. A net plunged into the depths. The fish was hurled up into the blinding sun and the heat, until it lay gasping amid the jewels and the pearls.

They fell upon it, white men and brown. A sharp knife was drawn. It sank deep into the flesh of the great fish, and no one heard its cry of pain as it was cut and divided, divided yet again and again, and pieces given to all who stood with eager, greedy hands outstretched.

I woke up, gasping, doubled over with pain, for the knife that had sunk into the fish seemed to have been drawn across my own body.

It was only a dream, I told myself again and again. But all day as I went about my work, the dream would suddenly catch me again, bringing a dryness to my throat and a dull ache, as from an old wound.

Elizabeth stared at me strangely. "Are you ill?" she asked.

"I didn't sleep well last night," I replied.

"The nights are getting cold."

"Didn't sleep well?" she asked. "Or do you mean you lay awake and couldn't sleep—perhaps you were troubled by thoughts. . . ."

"No," I said brusquely. "Go—go wash something. Go cook and carry water, since you do it so well." I had meant it as a jest, but it came out sharply. "I'm sorry," I said hastily, eager to ward off a scene or even tears.

"It's all right, William," she said, half hiding a secretive smile, and she hurried away to help Emme Merrimoth gather leaves and roots.

As evening fell, I became afraid of the night and the dream, which might return. I stumbled about, like a beggar staring into rich people's windows, watching in despair and loneliness. Chris Cooper and his friends spilled out laughter and stories as ale spills from kegs, and I envied them. The men with their wives, those with sons and brothers—I envied them. Nobody knows me! I thought in a sudden panic. If I were to die on this very spot, who would care? They would bury me without a sign, and auction off my knife, my breeches, my tin cup and the tortoiseshell. Where are all the treasures meant for me? They would divide up my goods just as they'd divided the body of that fish . . .

Horror struck, I stopped dead still.

"Evening, William," murmured Ananais.

"Feeling ill, William?" asked Brooke. "You look a bit pale."

I barely nodded to them. Panting, I walked faster

and faster, until I was nearly running, not even knowing whom or what I was seeking. Then I saw him sitting on a stump, and I cried out, "Master Rufoote! A word with you, please."

He bobbed his head rapidly, in lieu of a bow, and he waved me to an adjacent stump. "Sit down, my friend—fine evening. Is there some way I might be of service to you?" He looked at me briefly, and I knew he had already judged my despair.

I told him the dream in every detail, while he leaned toward me, encouraging me with nods and murmurings, "Quite so—and then?"

When I was finished, he asked the date of my birth. I told him, February 28.

"Pisces," he nodded. "Just as I thought. The sign of the fish."

"The—the fish?"

"Of course." Slowly he wrung his hands as if he were washing them. "What was the fish in your dream?" he asked, staring at me intently.

"It was I, myself," I said in a harsh whisper.

"Quite so. And you are in a state of confusion. It is quite common for Pisces, this state—and oh, how deep is your confusion, how low you sink at times. It is the weakness of your sign, this discouragement. Let a Pisces suffer a bad experience, and he does not forget. No—it plunges him into despair, and only slowly does he rise up again."

Yes, he was looking into my very soul, into my past and my future. I was afraid to see what he saw, but more afraid *not* to see. "What does the dream mean?" I whispered. "What must I do?"

"Pisces," he mused, with the slow washing movements of his hands, "Pisces can rise to great heights, if only they will not divide their efforts. Pisces can achieve happiness and honor in service to humanity. Teachers, preachers, doctors—these are Pisces at their best. Pisces are compassionate, sensitive. They cannot bear to watch or to cause suffering. And in them, too, is an artistic flair, a love for beauty."

Breathlessly I listened, gazing beyond him to the hundreds of stars that now showed themselves. The stars were like Holy Writ, undeniably true; my life was like an open book, for Rufoote to read.

"What must I do?" I asked again.

"Do not vacillate! Keep a steady course to your goal," he replied.

"My goal—the light in my dream—is that it? Is it a sign that I must be ready to gather treasure at Chesapeake, and not be put off by—by . . ."

"Perhaps. Other forces are warring in you, trying to divert you from your goal. But perhaps the golden light means treasure of a different sort, the golden joy of serving humanity."

"Roger Prat tells me I was called—" I paused, embarrassed, "to God's service."

"Perhaps. You see, the course is charted. You are only the instrument, and many signs give warning. Feelings, dreams—your greatest danger lies not in outward forces, but within yourself. You see, you have already served, but now you vacillate. You have brought us a heathen soul. . . ."

"I? I brought Manteo?"

"He is seen a great deal in your company. You and he are in harmony."

I nodded, bowed my head to humble myself. It was true. Manteo did speak to me in a different way from the other white men. With the others he used words awkwardly, as if he were pretending not to understand.

"I have watched you," Rufoote continued warmly, "acting out this destiny of service. You took pity on Elizabeth Glane."

"Reluctantly!" I admitted, for he knew—he knew me better than my own father.

"But you did it! And you have looked after young George, and now another heathen soul."

"Telana?"

He only stared at me intently, his eyes nearly as bright as the stars above him. Then he rose, placed his hand on my shoulder. "Follow," he said, "follow your course. Soon enough you'll discover the true meaning of that golden light in your dream."

I stood up, about to offer some payment, but he read my thoughts.

"Do not speak of it!" he said, hand uplifted. "We are meant to help one another."

FOURTEEN

LIKE MANY OTHERS, I had been sleeping out under the trees at night. Now it was time to build myself a winter shelter.

I decided not to join the men that day when they went to Wokokon to hunt. Most of the women went with them, equipped with large pots in which to render the fat of the deer and bears the men hoped to catch. I was glad for the opportunity to work alone on my hut. The air was sultry, and I'd sent Georgie off to rest. Lately he'd been seen often going or coming from the native village. The women shook their heads over it, and Mistress Jones had had words with him once or twice. But calmly Georgie went his own way, and I was just as glad he did not come to me for an opinion.

Happy in these minutes of rare solitude, I planned out my day. I'd finish these few boards, then bathe in the pool. Later I'd climb up to my plateau, and perhaps there I'd begin my letter to Bessie. Soon our ships would be sailing home, and I must send a letter to her.

Through the ringing of my hammer I heard a shout. Someone was beating the bushes, calling frantically.

"William, come quick!" Georgie, breathless and limping, shouted, "It's s-started, and Elizabeth said to fetch you. Mistress Merri-m-moth is shaking Mistress Dare to make her cry, and Agnes Wood says she'll kill it!"

"For God's sake," I shouted, trotting after him. "What's started?"

He stopped on the path, twisting his hands. "Mistress Dare is having her—her baby."

I ran like a thunderbolt. At the edge of the Dare hut I stopped, hearing the commotion from inside—a cry, a wail, a curse. I leaned against the doorway. Why hadn't I gone to Wokokon with the others? I hadn't the faintest notion what to do for a woman in childbirth—I'd never even seen a puppy born.

Again came the cries of a struggle. "Leave me— leave me! Elizabeth, don't let her . . ."

Agnes Wood burst out the door, covering her face with her apron. "It's no place for a woman," she wailed. "I told her! Oh, the poor babe, Lord take pity!"

"Elizabeth!" I called from the doorway. She ran toward me.

"William, you've got to *do* something."

"What can I do?" I shouted. Behind me I saw the stout shape of Emme Merrimoth, bent over Elinor, shaking her violently. With each shake she cursed the stubborn baby that would not be born.

A steady low moan from Elinor Dare rose to a piercing shriek.

"Do something!" cried Elizabeth. "Go get Mistress Archard. She'll know. She's had a child. Quick!"

"But all the women have gone. I—I'm not wanted here. It's woman's business."

She clenched her teeth. "Mistress Archard stayed behind with her babe. Go!" she screamed. "Go get her! Emme will kill that baby! I've seen it, how they pull until the little head. . . . It will be your fault. Go!"

I ran to Mistress Archard's cabin and found her preparing soap. I blurted out my message. She sank down in a chair.

"You must come now!" I cried.

"I? Oh, no." She shook her head slowly and gathered her baby up into her arms. "I cannot. No, William, I must not."

"You must! All the other women are gone. You must know about it. You've had a child."

She rocked to and fro and tears began to slide down her cheeks. "I cannot," she whispered. "I am cursed. *Cursed.* Whatever I touch—the child would be dead."

"It will die under the hands of Emme Merrimoth!"

"Mistress Merrimoth is a good woman."

"We need you!"

"Twice I tried," she whispered, rocking. "Twice I brought death. My own sister's child. And this precious babe is the only one left to me of three—do you understand?" She looked up at me, her eyes wide in agony. "Oh, William, I am *sorry*."

I left her there and stumbled down the path. Hearing voices, I peered through a clump of bushes. Murmuring and laughing, Telana and Quinsha were digging sassafras roots.

"Telana!" I ran to her. "Do you know about babies?"

She stared at me, half smiling, then whispered to her friend. "Yes," she said. "I know."

"Then come with me."

They followed, still murmuring and chuckling. But at the doorway of the cottage they stood mute and horrified.

The struggle had reached a fever pitch. Emme Merrimoth, gritting her teeth, shook at Elinor who writhed and screamed while she clutched a rope tied around her waist. Her body was encased in a blanket; only her head and arms were free, and her face was swollen in pain.

Telana strode into the room and stood squarely before Emme Merrimoth. "Out!" she shouted with a fierce gesture. "Out!"

Quinsha began a stream of scolding, waving her arms. Her round, good-natured face took on Elinor's own expression of suffering.

"Out!" Telana cried again. I hadn't believed her capable of such anger. I grasped Emme Merrimoth's arm, trying to pull her aside.

"Savages!" she spat. "You bring savages to the daughter of Governor White!" She sputtered in disbelief. "The child will be cursed, born with deformity." She planted her feet wide apart, and I knew her large bulk would not be moved without violence or spectacular diversion. Wildly I glanced around the room but found nothing to help me. I seized at the first thought and whispered to her, "Go to Mistress Archard. She is sick—dazed—*possessed*."

"You lie!" Emme Merrimoth screamed, lunging back to strike at me. But in that instant came a cry from the doorway. "Mistress Merrimoth!" There stood Joyce Archard, looking only half complete without the baby in her arms. In her stance and in her eyes I saw the tremendous effort that had brought her there, felt the enormity of her sacrifice. And silently I blessed her as she acted out her part. "Oh, please, please come quickly!" she implored, wringing her hands. Her mouth twisted, and clawlike her fingers grasped at the air. She ran, and Emme Merrimoth followed, screaming back, "Patience, Mistress Dare! There is yet time."

Gently Telana removed the rope from Elinor Dare's waist, untied the knot that held the other end to the bedpost. Deftly she loosened the blanket. Then she turned to me. "Out," she said firmly, and I gratefully obeyed.

The sun moved slowly across the sky while I sat

with my back against the cabin wall. This day of birth was drawn out beyond all reality—is it always so? I heard their murmurings from inside, distant and dreamlike. Quinsha came out, soon returned bearing an earthenware jar. She had been gone only a few minutes, but her movements seemed incredibly slow.

Then Elizabeth came out and sat down beside me. She spoke, and I marveled at the briskness of her tone, at the ordinary words. "It will be some time yet. Likely you'll want supper soon. We've a bit of meat left from yesterday, and biscuits."

I only shook my head, felt myself floundering in confusion, desperately recalling the fish who must not let himself sink. How could she think of food? Biscuits!

"They gave her some kind of medicine," Elizabeth continued. "Wine and root tea, I think. I tasted it. Master Dare will not be angry with me, will he? It was Elinor herself who ordered Emme Merrimoth away! What was I to do? She is my mistress, isn't she? I work for her. I'm bound to do as she wishes," she argued. "And you too—you saw what Emme Merrimoth was doing. You sent her away."

I could only stare at her.

"Well, they are good to her, and she is not screaming anymore," Elizabeth went on, rubbing her back. "Why is everything so hard? Oh-oh, it's horrible! I never want to . . ." She stopped, deeply flushed. "But they are good to her. They sing to her and hold her hands, and they seem to *know* what to do. Sometimes I forget that they are only savages."

"Don't use that word!" I said sharply.

"How cross you are lately, William. How changed. Perhaps it's all that bathing," she said scornfully.

"I? You're the one who's changed." I drew myself up now, faced her. "I've been meaning to speak to you since . . ."

"Elizabeth! Come!" Telana called from inside. Again the door was closed. I heard a single long cry. Then came a new voice, a faint trembling wail. It sputtered and choked, gasping feebly, and I imagined a meager flame wavering against the wind. But the cry grew stronger and stronger, until it became a lusty human sound, mingled with women's laughter.

When at last they called me in, I walked on tiptoe, grinning in spite of myself, feeling foolish and overlarge. Mistress Dare lay quietly with the tiny creature tucked in the crook of her arm. This red, raw little lump of life would grow into a boy with a name, a man with opinions.

"Come closer," Elinor Dare whispered. "I want to thank you."

"Congratulations," I whispered. "Is it? . . ."

"A girl. Her name is Virginia, because she is the first. Carry her for me, William, since neither her father nor her grandfather are here."

Before I could reply, Elizabeth had placed the baby in my arm. "All around the house," she reminded me, beaming, "out the door and back again."

How light she was, how frail! A hundred evils, a mere puff of wind could kill her in an instant. I must not stumble! A tight small fist emerged, waved as if making a claim. How strong—how strong is this life!

I returned, feeling unbelievably weary, yet proud in my accomplishment.

"I'll stay here until Master Dare returns," Elizabeth said. She wiped Elinor's face, tucked in the blanket with firm, confident movements, and all the while her face shone with a new light.

Outside the same glow touched Quinsha and also Telana. I could not speak, even to thank them. I reached out my hands. And suddenly, for the briefest moment, I felt Telana's hair brushing my cheek and her warm face close to mine.

Then I ran to the beach to await the hunters and cry out the news.

That night the ale flowed unstinting from the kegs, and every secret, private brew barely begun was offered to rejoicing. Healths were drunk, good wishes heaped upon everyone concerned. And somehow, as the cups were emptied and filled, certain deeds were forgotten and new ones put in their place. A toast to Mistress Merrimoth! A toast to the good woman who had delivered the Governor's daughter of a fine, healthy child.

I drained my cup, laughing and contented. And as we all watched and cheered, the Governor brought out his Journal and wrote, "On August 18 a daughter was born to Elinor, daughter of the Governor and wife of Ananais Dare."

* * *

Little Virginia was christened the following Sunday. Since I had been present at her birth and was the first man to carry her, I was named as godfather, beside John Sampson and Dyonis Harvie.

"By God," said Hugh, rolling his eyes, "you've a knack for being in the right place at the right time, William. How sweet it is to have friends in high places! Now I suppose you'll come and go at the Governor's house like a relative."

I smiled. "It was only a courtesy," and I reminded him, "You'd best prepare your letters for home."

The Lion and our flyboat were nearly ready to sail. I had carved the small figure of a deer for Bessie. Now, as I sat by the dim firelight over my letter, I didn't know where to begin. How could I explain this land to her? How could I even explain this new life to myself?

That afternoon I'd watched the sailors loading the ships with provisions. Suddenly it had seemed we were no longer so far from England or from Spain and the war that everyone said must come.

And if there were a war, might not all travel to the colonies stop? Night after night the men talked about it. In case of war, how would we get our supplies? All ships would be drafted into service. And if King Philip really did build himself an armada that could defeat our navy, Spain would be mistress of the seas. We would be totally cut off from our homeland.

The idea must have been at the edge of my mind since our landing. Now it obsessed me. I must send for Bessie now. Surely I'd proved my trust by looking after Elizabeth Glane. I made my way toward the Governor's house, looking up at the stars. Yes, it was all charted there. Destiny had placed Elizabeth Glane in my way, and I had accepted the challenge, which led straight to this moment. "Do not vacillate!" Rufoote's voice seemed to echo. I must not forget my first goal, to bring Bessie here and look after her.

Governor White sat at his table, checking over lists of supplies. As I approached him he looked up, pen poised. "Yes, William?"

"My sister Bessie," I began, "I've told you about her."

"Yes, yes."

"She is nearly ten years old. And very grownup for her age. You said I might send for her."

"Well, then?"

"I'm—I'm preparing a letter for her now. I want to tell her that she may come in the spring, with the supply ship."

"A child of ten?"

"My sister, Bessie. I'll care for her. She won't trouble anyone."

"And during the voyage?"

"You said there would be others coming. And Bessie—soon she'll be—I mean, sir, we are to become a permanent colony, and there are so few women here."

"A child of ten!" he exclaimed, laughing. "By God, William, do you plan to bring her as a bride for little Ambrose Viccars?"

"I only thought . . ."

He sighed. "We'll see. Right now I have worries enough. Two of the Assistants had agreed to return to England to purchase our supplies. Now none of them will go, not even Christopher Cooper, and he seemed so eager."

"I'll go!" I cried impulsively.

"Oh, William." He faced me with a sad, gentle expression. "It has to be an Assistant, or someone who . . ."

He broke off, and I felt ashamed of my torn shoes and the small knife that hung at my waist. What a wild, ridiculous idea. I was still a pauper, still uncounted.

"It must be an Assistant," the Governor repeated mildly. "Our representative will have to make a report to Sir Walter Raleigh, and there will be a great deal of business . . . I can't understand why Cooper refuses! Ah well, nobody is eager to face another ocean voyage, to leave his possessions . . . leave me. Leave me now to my work."

He motioned me to a place beside the hearth, and idly I began to sketch. Yes, pictures would be better than words, even my crude pictures of huts and hills and the pond.

I forgot time and place in my absorption, working with bits of charred wood, until I fell asleep on the floor. Abruptly I awakened to the morning and the sound of voices and a knocking at the door.

The group that now pressed forward looked as if they had spent a sleepless night planning for this moment. They were led by Thomas Stevens, the lawyer.

"A most urgent request, Governor," I heard him say. "We have met in all earnestness to discuss . . ." He cleared his throat. "Many of the colonists and Assistants, including myself, urge you most strongly to return to England yourself to see to the dispatch of our supplies. We have considered the matter from every side, and we feel that you yourself are best qualified to do this."

Ananais came from the back room to stand beside the Governor. His expression changed from approval to uncertainty, but he said nothing as Stevens continued with reasons upon reasons for his request.

At last the Governor said firmly, "I cannot go."

"If you will but consider. . . ."

"I have considered it. Listen, many of you came to the New World at my persuasion. If I left you now, some would say that I had deceived you, that I brought you here never really intending to stay."

"Nobody would slander you," Stevens protested. "You've brought your family here, and your possessions."

"And what would happen to my possessions while I'm gone? I don't like to mention it, but even while

I was on Croatoan for a mere two days, I returned to find some of my things—ah—mislaid."

"Surely your son-in-law will guard your things," Stevens said.

"That's the least of my concern," replied Governor White. "Neither is the thought of being separated from my family enough to make me refuse. But it is my responsibility to govern this colony. I can only do so by remaining here. You will have to choose among yourselves whom you will send to England."

The day passed in wrangling, while the Governor and Ananais stayed in their house. I wondered what was passing between them. Certainly, there would be a great chance for Ananais Dare to gain control of the colony while his father-in-law was gone. How could he not appoint his own son-in-law? And yet, how could he, with Stevens the wiser man, Sampson better liked, and even Roger Prat more highly regarded. I would not have wanted to be in the Governor's shoes.

The next morning, again, the Governor was confronted, this time by an even larger delegation. Elinor, just up from childbed, stood beside him, pale and silent. I stood outside among the others, wondering what choice she might make if she were asked, and I pitied her, realizing for the first time how very young she was, just twenty, I think.

"I bring you this petition," Stevens said loudly, "signed by nearly all the colonists." He held out the paper, then began to read it:

"May it please you, Her Majesty of England's subjects, we, your friends and countrymen, the planters of Virginia, do by these presents give all of you to understand that for the immediate supply of certain of our apparent needs, requisite for our successful planting in Virginia, we have unanimously and earnestly entreated, with incessant requests, John White, Governor of the planters in Virginia, to sail to England speedily to obtain the help and supplies aforesaid."

He drew a deep breath, and Elinor leaned wearily against Ananais.

The lawyer continued. "We are sure that he can perform this labor and will take the utmost pains for our sakes. Not once, but often, he has refused to go, bearing in mind our safety and the reputation and success of our expedition."

"Stevens!" the Governor called out, hands spread out as if to ward off the flow of words. But Stevens continued.

"But at last we have importuned him much against his will, to leave his government as well as his personal property in our hands and return to England on our behalf. Of his wisdom and fidelity in handling this matter," Stevens concluded rapidly, "as in all else, we do assure ourselves by these presents and beg you to concur this twenty-fifth day of August, 1587."

His proclamation ended, Stevens heaved a great sigh.

The Governor, Ananais, Elinor—all three

seemed caught in wax, their emotions bared for everyone to see.

At last the Governor held out his hand and took the document from Stevens. He said, "Very well. You leave me no other choice."

* * *

Only one day remained for the Governor to prepare himself. He was besieged by people begging him to carry back their messages and tokens. Late in the evening I rapped at his door and was bidden to enter. Papers and clothes were scattered everywhere; his heavy trunks were only half packed.

"Governor," I said softly, "my sister—may she come?"

He pressed his hand over his eyes for a moment, repeating, "Your sister?"

"Yes, Bessie Wythers," I exclaimed. "You'll find her at Master Taylor's if you consent . . ."

There came an urgent knock at the door, a hasty shuffling of footsteps, and Henry Rufoote appeared, holding a sheaf of papers. "A word with you, my Lord, a most vital matter," he said, bowing as he went. "I have just now finished, just in time." He pushed the papers at the Governor. "See how clearly it is written, wondrously clear! The constellations cross . . ."

"Compose yourself, my good man," interrupted the Governor.

"Your pardon, Governor," I broke in, "the matter of my sister." I could see the blue vein throbbing at the Governor's throat. "I have this letter for her.

May I tell her that she may come?"

The Governor gave me a fierce glance. Then his expression softened. "Yes, yes, very well. Tell your sister that I will fetch her and bring her to you, God willing."

"You see," Rufoote explained, pointing, "Tomorrow is the twenty-seventh day, and . . ."

"Thank you!" I cried. "Oh, thank you, Governor."

"William Wythers, go and write your letter! Now out with it, Rufoote. How can I help you?"

"Help me? In all humility, it is I who would help you. You see, it is a most portentous date, the paths intersect here—a time for caution, caution and reflection."

"I seem to remember your telling me that seven is my lucky number," said the Governor. "Tomorrow, being the twenty-seventh, should be a most fortunate time to begin my journey."

"Yes, ordinarily that would be so," cried Rufoote, "but there are other influences! I have taken the liberty of comparing Captain Ferdinando's horoscope with your own, and aside from that . . ."

"Rest easy then," said Governor White. "I've decided to sail on the flyboat with Captain Spicer. Thank you, my friend . . ."

"No!" cried Rufoote. "Begging your indulgence—the date is ill chosen, all the signs point to uncertainty, even catastrophe. Delay, my Lord, I beg you, delay but a day or two."

Rising, the Governor said firmly, "That I cannot

do. The ships are ready to sail. Just pray for us."

"Then, Governor, I implore you! At least heed this last. You must return to Virginia before the seventh month, before July."

"Of course," the Governor assured him, leading him to the door.

"Before July!" came the plea once again from outside, and the Governor sank down, shaking his head, half-smiling. "With everything else still to be done," he murmured, "thank Heaven I'm not a firm believer in the stars."

I prepared to leave as again I heard footsteps and a knocking. "Ah, the Assistants," said the Governor, rising. To me he said, "You may stay."

"I?"

"You write with a fine hand, as I've seen."

"Sir?"

"We will need someone to keep the Journal while I am gone. A scribe. Are you willing to serve?"

I was breathless, stunned.

"Someone," he continued, "removed from power, without enemies . . . are you willing?"

"Yes, yes, sir!" I said, wishing for dignity despite my trembling.

When the Assistants had assembled, John White told them of my position as scribe. "There being no objections," he added, "so be it." He handed me a quill and a new book.

In disbelief I sat there at the large table, trying to think the proper thoughts—who would be appointed to rule in the Governor's absence? What must I write in this book? But I thought of my father—what would he think to see me sitting here?—of my mother, and of Almighty God, praise Him! who had raised me to such estate.

Pride goeth before a fall, came the warning in my brain. Pay attention! Scribe is not nobility—but better, oh, a hundred times better than pauper!

". . . since you each have separate abilities," the Governor was saying, "it is my decision that you will rule jointly, as a council. Each man's vote will carry the same value. The majority will rule."

There was a long silence, while each of the Assistants weighed the effect of this astonishing decision. Then Cooper, averting his eyes, asked, "How long shall we hold the Governor's power?"

"Until my return next spring," the Governor replied.

"But suppose," persisted Cooper, "some fate should prevent it?"

The Governor's voice rose. "I intend to return! But—should something go wrong, and I be delayed, you shall decide by vote whom to appoint as Governor in my stead."

"When would this vote be taken?" Ananais asked.

"Give me until September of next year."

Dyonis Harvie motioned with his hand. Just two days earlier his wife had given birth. "Shall we move to Chesapeake in spring, regardless . . ."

"You'll have only the pinnace," the Governor replied. "To travel by land, I see now, would be dangerous, for many hostile tribes lie between here and

Chesapeake. Wait for the ships. But," he hesitated, "should you find it absolutely necessary to move from here, we should agree upon a sign, so I will know where to find you.

"If you should leave," he said heavily, "carve the name of the place into a tree. If you go in distress, also carve the sign of a Greek cross."

The meeting was over, and I gazed at the first entry I had written into the Journal. Following the stern emphasis in the Governor's tone, I had underlined the words, *"carve the name of the place into a tree."*

* * *

As they weighed anchor, a dozen sailors at the capstan of the flyboat were thrown and injured. They tried again, failed again. At last they cut the cable and let the anchor go. It was an evil omen.

FIFTEEN

IN THE HEAVY HEAT of September, we sat outdoors to catch the occasional breeze from the Sound.

The Governor had been gone for two weeks. When the master is absent from the house, everyone moves over to fill his place. So it was after Governor White left. For the first few days we set to work with the air of those who need to prove their faithfulness to duty. But now our village was finished, all but the frills, and we rested. Not that we were idle. But the first great wave of effort had been spent. There came a general sense of ease as we waited to gather in our harvest. But gradually this ease turned to restlessness. Even the children seemed noisier, more demanding.

"Mother! If William takes me, why can't I go?" Ambrose cried petulantly. "Please, please may I go, just this once?"

"Certainly not," Mistress Viccars retorted. "You just sit down there under that tree and get on with your letters."

"But Mother, Georgie Howe goes nearly every day."

The mother faced him, finger wagging. "And since when do we judge ourselves by those who are foolish and feeble-minded? Let Georgie Howe run wild, then. I'll have better for you, Ambrose Viccars. 'Twas not an easy thing for your father and me to come out here to this hellish wilderness." Angrily she slapped at the buzzing insect on her arm. "Finish your letters," she repeated more gently, "there's a good boy. Then you may play with Bobby and Tom."

Mistress Viccars took up her stitchery, mouth set as she pushed the needle through the heavy cloth. "William, you've no kin here," she began, "so I shall take the liberty of speaking with you as—as a mother. What you do influences others—like Ambrose. He thinks well of you, and I must admit that he would do well to follow your example of industriousness and—and service."

"Thank you, Mistress Viccars," I put in quickly, smiling.

"We all note with approval," she continued, "how you have looked after Georgie, dim though he is, still one of God's creatures."

"Mistress Viccars, he may be afflicted, but he is not . . ."

"But then," she said heatedly, "you run off and sit among the savages."

Roger Prat, having nailed down a barrel stave, strode toward us, hammer still in his hand. "Mistress Viccars," he said warmly, "we would all do well to take a leaf from William's book. He goes to the heathen daily, to bring them . . ."

I spoke out sharply. "I go to—to . . ." I stopped, confused. Why *did* I go? What did I find there that I couldn't find here, among my friends? "I go to watch over Georgie," I said, and my face burned.

"Every nation has its messengers," Roger Prat continued, and he put his hand on my shoulder. "William has a gift, a way of winning the confidence of the savages. And mark you, Mistress," he said sternly, "there may come a time when we need his ability."

Maurice Allen, cracking nuts between his teeth, moved closer to add, "It is ever well to have a friend in the enemy camp. Let me tell you, these savages all know what the others are doing. They have a signal system—God knows how it works. But they all know each other's movements, and I for one will not rest easy until we have the head of Wanchese on a spit."

Lord, I thought in distraction, must every private word become a public free-for-all? Must they forever divide me into little pieces, arguing over *my* motives?

Now others, ready for their noon meal, came to join in. Cooper's face was glazed with sweat, his breathing was heavy. "I say we move out before winter, while the advantage is ours. One does not wait for a snake to strike twice. Early begun, the battle is won," he added, obviously pleased at his choice of words.

"Could be," Hugh mused, only half in earnest, "we'd have time to take a brief journey to Chesapeake, to size up the land, as it were. Along the way we could hunt Wanchese." He turned to me. "Surely Manteo knows where he's hiding."

"I really couldn't say," I said coolly. "Why would Manteo know?"

"Because they all stick together," retorted Maurice Allen. "And mark me, when the time comes for choosing, it will be savage with savage, and never mind promises made. What's a promise to a savage, anyway?"

"Ther'll be no choosing sides," John Sampson said calmly, "and no warring. We'll stay put, get in our crop, and be ready for winter." He squinted to the distance, as if he could see winter moving slyly over the hills. "Oh, it's good sport to go adventuring when the weather's fine. But winter will tell what stuff we're made of."

We were silent, brooding. Winter would come; it might be harsh and even merciless, but it was hard to believe in winter while the sun poured over us.

" 'Tis sad and lonely to look out toward the harbor and see our ships gone," murmured Joyce Archard.

"We've still got the pinnace!" said Sampson cheerfully.

"If only they'd left us the flyboat instead," murmured Margaret Lawrence.

"Never mind, my sweet, I'll carry you to Chesapeake!" laughed Chris Cooper, and somehow it angered me unreasonably. Cooper could lay his hands on her, speak to her in the most unseemly, intimate way, yet nobody criticized *him!*

Maurice Allen flapped his arms at the mosquitoes, yelping, "Damnable beasts!"

"There's an herb," I said, "that the natives use to keep insects away. I have offered it to you," I added, "but it seems you'd rather be bitten than try it."

"Surely," laughed Cooper, "if that's the source of the stink on their flesh, I'd rather be eaten alive!"

"Next you'll have us go half-naked, I suppose," laughed Allen. Mincing, hands before his loins in comic imitation of the natives, he circled around, enjoying the shouts of applause.

Suddenly their faces seemed to close in on me, not white, but very red, mouths open too wide, voices too harsh and dissonant. Even their clothes were outrageous, white collars and knitted cloaks, shirts beribboned, embroidered, buttoned up high—no wonder they were sweltering in these unnatural, ridiculous clothes!

From a distance I caught Rufoote's gaze. "Steady," his eyes seemed to say. "Do not sink into confusion—do not be divided. Rise above these petty things, on to your goal."

I fought down my anger. Just yesterday Elizabeth had cried out at me, "Why are you always in such a temper?"

Later I made my way to the native village, telling

myself I was only going to fetch Georgie back. But as I walked between the trees toward the quiet huts, several of the little children ran to meet me, and their laughter was very gentle to my ears. Breathing deeply, I walked on past the men shaping their arrows and stretching skins, past the women and their cooking pots. Telana and Quinsha were murmuring together as they worked to soften the hide of a doe.

"William!" Telana rose in greeting, as always, and smiled. "Welcome!"

And it seemed somehow that an invisible circle widened, drawing me inside.

* * *

I had never really seen an autumn before—autumn, even more beautiful than spring. The evenings were crisp and filled with the scent of pine and lingering wood smoke from our last fires. The days were mild; shades of green turned to vivid yellow, gold, orange and scarlet; and leaves trembled on the trees. We took in our harvest of pumpkin, peas, squash and corn. We gathered nuts and honey. We hunted, then smoked long strips of meat. Soon our winter storehouse was full.

My house was finished now. My "garden" was wild sassafras and holly shrubs. I'd thought briefly of planting the flower seeds I had brought from home, to leave something here after we had gone to Chesapeake. But—I was reluctant to change the land. It had taken us in, the way a river takes drops of water. After we left, our tracks would soon be covered; the wilderness would reclaim its own. I decided to save my seeds for Chesapeake.

My house had only one room, but I took pride in the sturdy walls and the fireplace. Elizabeth came to see it. Admiringly she caressed the wood, examined the shelves.

"It's a fine house," she said softly. "It's small—but not too small!" she added quickly. "Why, two or even three people could sleep here."

"Yes," I said carelessly. "Georgie can sleep here when he wants to, and Hugh and Clement can bring their bedding to keep us company."

She stiffened. "Georgie and you—oh yes," she said with heavy sarcasm. "I suppose you'll sleep on mats, like two savages!"

She stamped out, slamming the door behind her. What right had she to slam *my* door? Angrily I ran to see—had she damaged the wood? No, I had built it well, but I was angry just the same, and a short time later, when I met Telana, she sensed my mood.

At last I told her about Elizabeth and her frequent outbursts. To my surprise, Telana only smiled.

"What is it?" I asked. "Has Elizabeth spoken to you? Have I done something?"

She laughed and murmured something in her own language. I could only gather that it was another of her many proverbs, but she would not repeat it. Some things could not be translated to my complete understanding. This was partly because the Indians' concepts of time and truth were different from mine. I came to understand that one's idea of time does influence one's idea of truth. Manteo could say, "I do not know Wanchese," and it merely meant, "I do not know him *now*, for he has changed." It implied that he might change yet again, for according to the Indian way, everything and everyone changes according to season. On the other hand, when a white man said, "That person is dim-witted," the label was applied from then on for all time.

I learned these things as daily I went to the native village with Telana, for now that our harvest was in, my time was more free. Soon the women would look up at my approach, offer me a taste from their ever-steaming dishes. The children began to take my hands to show me this or that. Even the young braves began to walk beside me, or to spread out a mat and spend the afternoon in conversation.

At first Telana interpreted everything. But gradually I was able to mix the Indian words into my speech. And this was all they wanted—words, stories. They no longer asked about the "fire stick," "the glass that sees" or "glass that looks far." I owned neither gun nor mirror nor telescope.

"No matter," said Telana. "You have yellow hair they like to see, and you have stories. They say, 'make stories!' They listen. Talk long!"

I laughed. How odd, this notion, "talk long!" They were never in a hurry. How was it, I asked Telana, that they had all this time just to sit and listen to stories?

Telana sighed, wrestling with the explanation.

"We have time," she said at last, "because nobody took it away to count. Your people put time into the box that counts. So it does not belong to you anymore."

As I told one story after another, the hours did fly—time *did* belong to me. Sometimes I remained so long that Telana cooked for me, and I ate supper with the young men. Then they would tell me their legends—stories of the gods and their miracles, of men and their daring. Soon I could understand most of it without help from Telana. She found it most natural that I should learn her language. "You have gift of many tongues," she said simply, "like Manteo."

They did not care whether my stories were new, or the same familiar ones repeated. I reached back into my memory for all the fables and stories I'd ever heard. They listened raptly. I told them about my parents, my home in London, the half-forgotten episodes of my childhood. They listened, entranced.

"Tell again," they pleaded, "of brave chief (my father) climb wall of stone, fall down hard, try again."

They liked this tale of daring, and I began to understand the courage of my own father.

And then I told them the beautiful, sacred stories of the Crucifixion, of Christ's birth, of His words of wisdom and love.

"Tell again," they begged, "your *Kewas* go to *Mohomny*. Tell again, arrows in his hands and side, he not die."

I invited them to the next Sunday service, and Roger Prat was joyous. But most of them were too shy to come. "Bring Book to us," they said. So I brought them the Book, and they pressed it to their faces, exclaiming, "Now we not die!"

Earnestly I explained that with Christ their bodies might die, but their souls would have life eternal, and they said knowingly, "Yes, yes, is same our gods."

"No!" I cried. "It is not the same." And I labored to choose just the right words to make them understand, all the while thinking that I—*I* was surely sent here for this, my own crusade. Silently I prayed, "God, give me the wisdom to teach them. Help me to open their hearts to Thee."

And then they said, "You like, we pray to your Christ."

"*Only* to Him!" I said sternly, envisioning a glorious Sunday of mass christenings, the end of suspicion between us and the natives, the beginning of a truly grand harmony.

But they smiled, shook their heads and said, "We pray many gods. *Te tab.* We your friend. Take your god, too. It is good. More gods, more good. Manteo take your god, still pray to *Kewas.*"

I hadn't the heart to tell Roger Prat.

*　*　*

"Whatever do you find to *do* there?" Hugh asked again and again. "What draws you? The woman?"

I took him with me once or twice. The legends bored him. The food made him ill, he said. He traded a cap for a spear, but could not learn how to use it. Finally he traded it with Jane Pierce for a blanket. "Well, you deserve a bit of fun," he said at last. His face took on an eagerness. "That girl is quite taken with you, I expect. Tell me," he whispered, "does she ever remove her cloak?"

My heart was pounding. I held back an answer.

"I have seen her eying my beard," he continued, stroking his rough cheeks. "Seems to me you could put in a good word for your friend."

In one blind instant of fury I brought my fist smashing against his chin, throwing all my anger against him. Astounded, he reeled back, then dizzily stumbled toward me, and we pounded at each other like two animals, until blood spurted from my nose and mouth, and his flesh felt soft under my knuckles. At last we lay on the ground, silent. Then, dazed, he said, "I didn't know, William."

That night we sat up late, talking, and he said in a low, husky voice, "I am afraid for you, William. But this sort of thing—" he waved his hand vaguely, "look, I've known you since you were a moppet. This will pass, and nothing need be said. This is all new, and you are growing manly."

"You misunderstand," I said heavily. "Nothing— nothing like that has happened."

"Oh, well, then ..." he clasped my arm and began to talk about Chesapeake. "I've heard the savages there wear long ropes of real pearls around their necks. The children play with gold nuggets as toys."

That night again I dreamed about the river and the great fish, but this time his body was hacked only into two pieces.

*   *   *

Each afternoon the wind came whistling in from the Sound a little earlier. Low, chilling fog lasted a little longer each morning. But we were ready for winter. Our woodpiles were high. Our cabins had been chinked. Our storehouse was full, and we were at peace.

In the middle of the night the sound rang out— the bell! The bell clanged hysterically, clanged us awake, called us out into the cold, shouting, terrified. We ran out in our nightshirts to meet a whirling mass of flames, to hear their roaring, then the thunder sound of gunpowder going up in a gigantic burst.

Trembling with shock and cold, I stood mutely, watching with the others while the fire consumed our winter provisions. Then the cry went up, the shouting and wailing. "Our winter stores! Our powder!"

Ghostly white shapes streaked through the darkness, emerged with guns and swords and shouts for pursuit! Pursuit! But the marauders had long since fled.

The bell had brought the natives running. They stood back, watching, until the smoke began to settle down. I saw Telana and Manteo press forward. "William!" she cried, and strangely her face was calm, only her eyes held sorrow, then gratitude. "You are safe!"

A shout began at the scene of the fire, spread outward to the crowd. A burned body lay in the rubble. Who? Who was not accounted for? The body was charred and twisted, but the brother of the dead man knew.

"Henry Berry. Muster Captain's brother." Whispers changed to shouts. "Henry Berry! Oh, my God."

* * *

The seven Assistants hastily gathered, shouted out to the milling crowd, "Yes, yes, but we must plan our strategy!" They gathered around the table, and I, still in my nightshirt sat over the Journal. All of us in that room knew it had already been decided. None of the seven, even if they wished it, could quench this flaming demand for revenge.

"You will write down what happened," Ananais told me sternly. "Then, our decision."

They all nodded soberly, and Dyonis Harvie put out the useless question, "Do we march?"

"It's not a question of whether!" shouted Cooper. "We all agree!"

"But where," said Sampson, "and when?"

They sent for Manteo and Richard Berry. Then Ananais closed the door against the milling crowd outside.

In turn they questioned Manteo, and he replied word by word, awkwardly.

"Who did this, Wanchese?"

"Wanchese."

"How do you know?"

"His spear."

"What spear—what are you talking about?"

"By trees, near bell. Spear with two feathers. Old sign of Pemisipan." He laid the spear across the table, pointed to the sign burned into it, two broken arrows."

"All right," shouted Richard Berry, pacing. "Where would they go now? Do they have a permanent camp?"

"Perhaps Skicoak," replied Manteo. "Some come from there."

"Listen," cried Cooper, lunging forward. "You *know*—don't pretend ignorance with us. We sit here while you ponder 'perhaps.' We should be marching out!"

"Perhaps Pomiock," Manteo continued slowly. "South."

"What the devil—he's lying!" shouted Cooper. "They'd have to cross the Sound to Dasamonquepeuk. I say we move out, and we'll take some savages with us. From there they'll track him down."

"What makes you so sure they'll lead us?" asked Stevens.

"There are ways," said Richard Berry, "such as Governor Lane employed." He put his hand to his sword.

And Manteo continued, as if he hadn't heard them. "Perhaps Chesapeake."

A change came over all their faces at the word "Chesapeake," a pause, a gasp that was felt rather than heard.

"Why Chesapeake?" demanded John Sampson.

"Some say maybe Wingos seek Chief Powhatan near Chesapeake. Ask Powhatan to join in make war against white man."

"Most likely they're gone to Chesapeake," called out Dyonis Harvie. "They prize the black pearls from there, don't they?"

"But isn't it likely they'd go home and settle in for winter?" put in Sampson.

"Perhaps Chawanook," nodded Manteo.

"Look, while we're sitting here supposing," cried Cooper, "that savage can be half way to Chesapeake! They're headed north, north to Chesapeake!" He pounded his fist on the table.

"Chesapeake!" they shouted, even Roger Prat; and John Sampson nodded, "Well, perhaps it's Chesapeake, then."

They would not wait for scouts to go ahead. They would not detour, but move straight on, on to Chesapeake.

"And Manteo stays here!" shouted Cooper between clenched teeth.

"Obviously," said Stevens, "some of the Assistants must remain here to govern the colony, otherwise . . ."

It was decided, and written into the Journal. Four would go, three would remain. I wrote, "The Assistants voted to send an army in search of the Wingos to Chesapeake. Those Assistants remaining on Roanoke to govern the colony are Roger Prat, Thomas Stevens, Ananais Dare."

* * *

Mistress Harvie, holding her infant, begged her husband not to go.

"Hush, wife," he stopped her. "Have you no pride? Obey me. Go back to the house. I will return, and when you count the treasure I bring, you'll never weep again."

We had held out a portion of our gunpowder in a smaller storehouse at the other end of our settlement. Now the men filled their pouches, and Richard Berry went among them, his eyes blazing.

"Yes, yes, fill your pouches with powder; and when they're empty, we'll fill them with jewels. I'm not one to cheat my soldiers of their pay! But first we'll take the heads of those bloody pagans. Yes, we'll carry their heads to Chesapeake! Fill your pouches with powder. A fair exchange, eh, powder for pearls?"

Hugh grasped my arm. "William! You'd best borrow a harquebus."

"Hugh, I'm not a soldier."

"What difference?" he cried. "Captain Berry says the more the better—even Tom Smart's going." He lowered his voice. "I've no doubt we won't look too hard for those savages. Don't you see? We'll be the first to reach Chesapeake . . ."

"Is it a battle then," I cried, "or a treasure hunt?"

"William, even Manteo says Wanchese did this."

"But nobody knows where he's gone," I retorted.

"To Chesapeake, of course! Listen, who knows what could happen if we wait. Wanchese would have more time to gather his strength. William! For

God's sake, this is what we have waited for! Even Clement's going."

"Hugh!" I felt like shaking him. "Wouldn't it make more sense to send scouts ahead?"

"I'm not the captain," Hugh said angrily. "But I haven't lost my nerve, either. Stay here then, but don't ask me later what happened to all those grand dreams of yours. Don't you even remember why we came?"

"I never came to slaughter savages!" I shouted, but the lie caught in my throat. "I—Godspeed, Hugh," I said, embracing him quickly.

He grinned at me. "I'll bring you a token anyway," he said. "Ho! Mistress Pierce," he called. "You're coming with us then?"

"What else?" she called back, heaving a satchel over her shoulder. "Won't you be needing someone to cook your supper?" Her hands fluttered eagerly, and her eyes danced, as if she could already feel and see the rich tokens she would gather.

Laughing, calling, carrying a basket, Margaret Lawrence caught up with her. I heard her breathless voice, "Jane, I've packed some extra liniment—have you got plenty of soap?"

I gazed in disbelief at how eagerly everyone ran to collect their things, like farmers bound for a day at the fair. I saw John Brooke rocking back on his heels, watching too. "Even women," he muttered, shaking his head.

"If they were bound for justice," I began, "only that. . . ."

"I know, I know," Brooke nodded.

John Sampson rushed past, whirled around to ask me, "William, you'll mind my tools while I'm gone?"

"Of course."

"Brooke, will you take heed of young John? My son thinks I'll conquer them single-handed," Sampson said, smiling slightly. "Well, I'm not a soldier," he said earnestly, "but I won't hold still for murder."

And Dyonis Harvie spoke of the women and children who must be protected against future attack.

And Chris Cooper said it was known for certain by the eight native scouts that Wanchese had fled to Chesapeake.

And Roger Prat raised his voice and his hands in prayer asking God to bless these brave men and their cause.

Hard faced, straight as a ramrod, Richard Berry stood beside the remains of his brother, which had been laid on a litter for everyone to see.

The brass bell mingled with the trumpet call and the cry, "Move out! To victory!"

SIXTEEN

NOW IT WAS DECIDED that a wall must be built, and with so many of our good men gone it was a heavy task. Day after day our axes rang out as we cut down the tallest trees to make a fort. Each stout post was sharply pointed on top and set close to the next. The arbor doorway was fitted with a heavy gate, and behind it we built a tall watchtower.

This took several weeks. By the time we were finished, the days were getting cold. We began to rebuild our storehouse. Then came the discouraging task of trying to fill it. We were clumsy fishermen, unskilled trappers. Game was scarce, and our supply of gunpowder nearly exhausted. As for trade with the natives, most things of value had already been traded for odd trinkets; and what food the natives had gathered, they would need for themselves. Also, since we had built the wall, they were reluctant to approach us.

A puzzling change came over many of our colonists, and I cannot say exactly what caused it. Perhaps it was fear of approaching winter—or the fact that we were fewer in number—or just the wall itself. Men who had been industrious became idle, whiling the hours away over dice and cards. Tom Stevens suddenly fell to writing his memoirs and would not leave his hut, except to refill his pitcher with mead. Roger Prat feverishly fashioned more barrels than we could possibly use. Following a bout of this frantic activity, he would sit for hours over his Scripture. Then suddenly he would take to the open places, wandering for days at a time. Whether he was seeking game or visions, no one knew, but as far as I could see, he never found either one.

Decisions of government—who should stand watch? how should food be divided?—and all the many disputes between individuals were brought to Ananais. He would hem and haw, ponder and pace, announce his decision, then change it again. Thus most of his time was spent in his house, and whenever I saw him, his face was creased with anxiety.

The work of building and repair kept me at the fort most of the time. But I carefully saved the hours of late afternoon for myself, yearning all day for that time. The wall oppressed me.

When the time came each day, I would run through the trees to the native village. There, out in the open, I could breathe. There I was able to work so steadily, so deftly with bits of wood, that I would carve a bowl in a few hours, while I told stories to the children. But one day only half the usual number of children appeared.

"There is great sickness," Telana told me, "new sickness. Many children have it."

Several of the braves were going out to hunt, she said. "They give meat to the gods, and our little ones will get well."

I watched them bring in their kill and give half of it as a burnt offering, and I thought of our empty storehouse.

From the beginning, Manteo had been willing to teach me everything—except how to shoot with a bow and arrow. He had made endless excuses; our fire stick was strong enough; to shoot with a bow and arrow required training since childhood. I had let it pass. I could understand that Manteo needed to save something. One doesn't easily give his ultimate weapon to a stranger.

But now our need was desperate. If I could learn to use the bow and arrow, and then teach others, we might yet survive the winter.

"Manteo," I said firmly one day, "I ask you to teach me to use the bow and arrow."

He hesitated only a moment, then said, "Yes. I will try."

So after that, early every morning, before the others were awake, I'd slip away to meet Manteo in the meadow. He was an exacting teacher. My arms and shoulders ached from drawing the bowstring again and again. And each time the arrow wobbled and wavered, missing its mark entirely, or it broke into pieces when my careless aim sent it flying into a rock.

"No," Manteo would say soberly. "Try again."

I lost count of how many arrows I lost or broke. I became furious and impatient with myself, cursing my clumsy fingers, while Manteo's only comment was, "No. Try again." To him the thing was all wrong or all right—nothing between.

Then after many hours and many days, I suddenly felt a difference. I felt a firm, sure release. The arrow landed with a *thunk* straight at the target. Manteo clapped me on the shoulder, beaming. "Good! See, it was in you to do this," he explained, taking no credit at all for my new skill.

From that day on, in the early mornings, we went out together stalking rabbits, porcupines, squirrels, and finally deer. These were among the happiest times of my life. As we hunted, I learned to hear the sound of a stream and to judge its course and distance long before we came upon it. I learned to search for droppings and tufts of animal hair, to read the countless clues that would lead us to meat. I was astonished that my feet could step so softly, that my eyes could see so keenly, that I didn't tire. I felt different—new.

Manteo must have felt it too, for one day he remarked, "If you were one of my people, you would get a new name."

Shortly after this, one of the little boys came up to me, pulling at my hand, and spoke excitedly. I understood him to say, in Indian language, "Now I know what your name means! In your tongue *Will-iam* means *Golden Arrow.*"

He would not accept any other explanation, for to his way of thinking my "true" name had at last been revealed. The Indians watch and wait. What sort of person is this? Patiently they wait, until the answer presents itself. With it, the name is spoken; but just as a person can change, so can his name. A slow, clumsy boy can change from "Little Turtle" to "Swift As The Rabbit." The name has nothing to do with a person's birth. He may be the son of a chief; still, he must prove his own nature. A name—any name, carries its own value, and no person is mocked or shamed for it. One young fellow was called "Lazy By The River," and his people merely said with a smile, "It is his way."

Strangely, when I was happiest in the wilderness, I'd get a flashing memory of my life in England. Was Rochester the same town I'd left behind? Was I the same person now as then? Now I could ask these questions without being afraid, but with a sense of wonder.

I recalled, from those distant days at Dame Broody's, the sampler on her wall that said,

> *"Full wise is he*
> *Who himself knoweth."*

Perhaps this was the greatest prize that any man could win—to know himself fully.

* * *

Sometimes at night I was seized with restlessness.

I'd hear the wind pushing against my cabin door. Then I'd think of Hugh and the others. They had been gone for over four weeks, and we hadn't heard anything. Had they already reached Chesapeake, and were their pouches filled with gold and pearls? Had I been foolish and worse—cowardly—for staying behind?

When I couldn't sleep, I would sit up later and paint. Telana's cousin, Tequinon, had showed me how to press and boil a certain root, which yielded a brilliant blue color. Thus I began to use pigment, enlarging my supply with the juices from berries, leaves, squash and walnut shells. Manteo helped me make several fine brushes from the hair of rabbits and deer, and from turkey feathers.

I painted the streams where Manteo and I had hunted. I tried to paint the children who sat at my feet listening to stories. I was never fully satisfied, but the visions of how I might yet render it kept me going. I showed my work to nobody, except Telana.

She would say, "Yes, it is so. There, the sun is just going down." She was delighted that a scene, once captured on paper, would never change.

"Make me a picture of you," she begged. "Then, in many seasons, when I am old, I can still see you."

I laughed at the idea. "I'm not good enough to make a picture of myself. But—but you! I could try to make a picture of you."

She smiled and said, "I will like it."

I attempted dozens of sketches of Telana. They were all wrong, stiff and sober.

She would sit very still for me, and I would study her features carefully, but I was unable to catch that certain hint of laughter in her eyes or any of the countless expressions that passed over her face in rapid succession when she spoke.

"I can't do it," I said at last, discarding another sketch. "It's all wrong. Even the paper seems too stiff."

"Sometimes my people make marks on white bark," she offered. "It is soft, but strong."

"Birchbark! Yes, I think I might do it—I'll try."

"The bark must be taken a certain way, with a sharp shell."

"Will you show me?"

"Yes. There is a place beyond the village where the birch trees grow thick and strong. The bark is very white and shines in the sun."

When the day came that I had some time to spare from my tasks, and I asked Telana to take me to the birch grove, she shook her head.

"Not this day."

"But you told me it must be cut before the rains begin."

"I am not going into the village today," Telana said, shaking her head firmly.

"Today I have time," I insisted. "Telana, take me. I hear your people singing a new song," I said, gesturing toward the sound that rose from the Indian village. "Take me. I want to learn it."

"It is not new," she replied, her eyes downcast.

"It's new to me. And you promised. . . ."

"Not today."

"Are you not well?"

"I am well."

"Come on, then," I said, firmly taking her arm. As we walked past the spring, Mistress Jones and Mistress Viccars looked up. I greeted them both, but they only stared at me, tight lipped.

I kept my hand tightly on Telana's arm. I'd never known her to be so stubborn before, dragging her feet, her expression sullen. At last, in exasperation, I burst out, "Telana! This is impossible. I won't *drag* you. I've asked you to take me. You say I am your friend!"

Then, wordlessly, she led the way, no longer resisting. But her head was still bowed, and her arms hung stiffly at her sides.

As we neared the village, the new song, with its wildly exciting beat, hastened my steps. For a moment I thought that it might be part of a sacred and secret ceremony. Perhaps I had no right to be there. But then I saw several of our planters sitting around the ceremonial circle, staring intently toward the center. The next instant there appeared a masked face, much larger than life, and so grotesque that I gasped aloud.

"Come away!" Telana pleaded, covering her eyes.

But the sight of the horrible mask held me spellbound, the frenzied singing drew me closer, until I moved into the very midst of it all. I couldn't speak. I couldn't even take my eyes away.

I stood, rooted to the spot, seeing the evil that

man is capable of performing—and of watching.

"Who is he?" I whispered at last.

"A captive found plundering," came Telana's muffled reply.

"How—how long—will it go on?"

"Two days or three. As long as he can live."

Only the captive did not scream. Those who watched, and those who applied each freshly devised torture, screamed for him.

"They could kill him with a single arrow!" I cried.

"They give him a chance to die well."

Blindly I fled, far into the forest, until I stumbled into the grove of white trees and clung to one of them, feeling my whole body heave and shake.

"William! William!" Telana ran to me. Her face was moist with tears. "I did not want you to see! Why did you come? You will think only of this. In your country men do not . . ."

"Leave me," I told her. And I was sick there alone, and much later I walked the long way around the edge of the island. I went inside the fort, inside my own small house, and for five days I went no further than the bristling wall we had built.

Yet the wall could not keep out the sounds that raged in my head. Echoing over these came the real sound of the natives' song that went on and on, day and night. On the third day the song changed. It was mournful, muffled and slow, and the drums throbbed heavily.

I was not aware of sleeping, only of waking up to confront that terrible sight anew each time. And each time it was just as vivid as the first.

Those five days passed for me as days pass for a person sick with fever. My mind wandered crazily back and forth—back to things I'd heard as a child and only dimly understood, back to our landing on Roanoke, on to the days on Croatoan when I first met Telana. I remembered first seeing Manteo, my fear of him, then knowing him and calling him my friend.

Again and again I relived those afternoons of talking with Telana, sitting with the children, stalking the hills with Manteo. And gradually I stepped back from my own visions and saw myself doing all these things, stepping into the New World with the expectation of an immortal soul entering Paradise.

Paradise! Again came the ugly scene of torture, and from far, far in the past I remembered a day in London, when I had sat in our parlor while my mother was mending. I might have been five or six. She had been speaking to me of God and prayers, as she often did, talking softly as she sewed.

"But where is heaven?" I'd cried out, longing to see it, for her smile and her gentle voice made it all seem so real and reachable.

She laughed softly, and I persisted, "Is it across the river? If I sail down the river to the end, will I see it?"

"No," she had said, putting down her needle and motioning me to come close. She put her hand under my chin, looking half serious, half teasing. "No, it is not at the end of the river. You'll find no heaven in this life at all, William. So you must just be good and say your prayers and wait until God calls you. But listen, William, and don't look so sad. God gives us other things, right here, things so good that they're almost like heaven. Things that give us a small look at what heaven might be like."

"What things?" I demanded.

"Duty," my mother said. "And most of all love."

I saw myself now; my thinking was just the same as that silly boy I had been, searching for heaven at the end of the river. So, this was not paradise. It was a wild and savage land, with people who could be unbelievably cruel. Even the word "savage" has a brutal ring to it. But—but there was another side, too, the side Telana and Manteo had shown me. And now I thought again of Telana, how she'd wept and said, "In your country men do not . . ."

Poor Telana—reared on legends. She still somehow connected the white man with the gods. What must her visions of England be? Paradise, no doubt, a paradise where people did not torment or kill one another. In all my stories about England I hadn't mentioned the public floggings, the gallows, the tower prison.

The Indian drums still throbbed out their low, mournful chant. What must Telana be thinking now, except that I'd judged *her* by what I'd seen, and that I found her evil, too, and hated her.

Finally I couldn't bear it any longer. It was nearly sunset when I ran down the path that linked the fort with the village. The drums urged me to run faster still, until I came to the ceremonial ground. The scene was totally different from the last time. The medicine man was doing a shuffling dance around the fire, flinging in bits of tobacco. Mourners followed him, echoing his chant, and I caught the words, "new sickness . . . strange plague . . . sweeping like fire . . . consume our offering, oh gods, and let our people live. . . ."

As I passed the huts, I saw with a shock that many of the doorways were sealed and the wall matting turned down firmly so that no light could enter. It was their custom, in times of illness, to seal their homes to prevent the entry of still more evil spirits. In time of sickness they made no fires and cooked no food, but depended on the offerings of their neighbors.

Telana! Her hut was at the far end of the village. I passed a small boy holding a bow and arrow. "Where is Telana?"

"Her house."

"Inside?"

The child had disappeared, engrossed in his game.

"Let her be outside!" I prayed silently. "Let her be sitting by her fire, grinding corn, please, let her be well!"

I passed the burial hut, where mothers and fathers sat wailing over their dead children.

Telana! Let her house be open. Let her be well!

I saw her then, just as I had that first time in Croatoan. She was moving back and forth as she ground the grain, humming softly to herself. For a moment I stood back, just watching her, just letting myself know that I loved her. I loved her! I wanted to rush out, take her in my arms, hold her close. But I approached slowly, knowing that she would hear my footsteps, as she did.

She moved only her eyes, watching as I crossed my arms over my chest in the native way of greeting. I sat down on the mat, the way Manteo had taught me.

"Telana." I nodded my head slightly.

"William." She nodded in return.

"Are you well?"

"Yes."

"And Manteo?"

"He has gone to Croatoan to give warning of the sickness."

"Telana, whose meal are you preparing?"

"Only my own."

"Is there enough for two?"

"There is always enough for a friend. Wait—I will serve you."

"No," I said. "I would have you eat with me."

Her color deepened, and in confusion she said, "Oh, William, you know I cannot. It is the way of my people that . . ."

"I know the way of your people," I said, looking deep into her eyes. "I would have you eat with me."

Suddenly her eyes filled with tears. I went to her and held her close, close against me. "Come with me, Telana," I said, taking her hand. "There is a place I want to show you. I've always gone there alone, but now . . ."

Hand in hand we passed through the village, then circled around the fort through the thick pines until we reached the rocky slope. I took her hand to bring her up to the plateau. Together we looked down at the cliffs, the beach below, the water and the forests beyond.

Never again would I see the sun setting in such glory. The sun was a ball of flame, touching the water with pink and gold, until the sky turned lavender, then deep blue purple. And Telana, watching it, reflected all that I felt as I gazed at her, until I drew her into my arms, and we kissed.

Kissing her hair, her face, her warm, beautiful mouth, I murmured over and over, "I love you, Telana. I love you."

"I love you, too," she whispered, looking up at me, and she was weeping. Then firmly she repeated the words, "I love you, William, oh I do."

I smiled. "Why is it that words of love make you cry?"

She shook her head, smiling and weeping together. "I don't know. Maybe because we waited so long."

We remained together on the hill until the water seemed to slip away into darkness and the stars shone high.

Hand in hand then we walked down the slope and to the village.

"Shall I cook for you now?" Telana asked.

I grinned. "I'm not hungry anymore."

"I know."

We walked on in silence, while the low chant of the mourners came closer. Now our way was lighted by the fires and the moon. "Some of my people say that . . ." Telana hesitated, "that this plague is brought by the white man."

"Do you believe it?"

"How can I, when I love you? But they say that your people bring this sickness because of the burning of your storehouse, and to avenge the murder of your friend."

"Why would we avenge ourselves on the people of Roanoke?" I reasoned. "They are our friends."

She sighed and continued with difficulty. "Some say that the white man thinks of all Indians as one."

"Who says these things?" I demanded.

"The priest, Harawok," Telana said. "Is it true, William?"

"You know it isn't true for me," I told her. "But the others—I guess some of them do think that way. And some of your people think all white men are the same."

"Yes," she whispered.

"We're not gods, Telana. Surely you know that."

She laughed. "I know that. I wouldn't want you as a god, but the way you are—a man."

"Then you must know," I continued, "that we have no power to bring sickness. Only gods can do that."

"Harawok says you bring sickness with the fire stick."

"It's not possible. Telana, do you believe me?"

"I love you, William. I believe. But—but Harawok says more. He says that the white man can make sickness strike or stay away. He knows that I am your friend, and Manteo, too. Harawok says it is because of this that Manteo and I have not been struck with the sickness."

"He thinks that I have the power to protect you from it! Then who protects Harawok? Why hasn't *he* caught the sickness?"

"Harawok doesn't speak of this."

"Well, I'll speak of it!" I exclaimed angrily. "Harawok wants to make trouble between us. His own medicine has failed, so he blames the plague on us."

We had come to her hut. "I wait for tomorrow to see you," she said, lifting aside the matting from her doorway. Then she came forth again, frowning, and asked, "Tell me, William, why is it that the sickness does not go beyond the wall your people have made?"

"I don't know," I admitted. "I really don't."

I walked back on the same road I'd traveled dozens of times, but my way had never been so light. I felt giddy and powerful all at the same time. I felt Telana close beside me again, her hair, her mouth, her body, her voice telling me that she loved me, and I ran with sheer joy, thinking, *this small part of heaven!*

But there was something I had to find out this very night. I made my way to Doctor Jones's house and knocked loudly. "William Wythers! We haven't seen you about lately."

Mistress Jones wiped her hands on her apron and led me inside. "What brings you? I hope it's not sickness, for the doctor is already tending . . ."

"Someone's ill? What is it?" Immediately I thought, if it were the same plague that had struck the natives, Harawok couldn't get away with his lies anymore. I was aghast at my own selfish feeling of relief. "Who is sick?" I asked.

"I know nothing," Mistress Jones replied. "But I've heard that there is sickness among the savages."

"Yes. Many of the children have died."

"Our people are wise to stay away from them," she said. She rushed to the door at the sound of her husband's footsteps.

The doctor nodded to me, threw off his cloak and sat back wearily. "Fetch me something to drink, wife," he commanded, and she rushed to obey.

He turned to me; his eyes were bloodshot. "William?"

"This—sickness," I began. "Is it the same plague that's struck the natives?"

"The same. It begins with a burning in the throat and a pain above the eyes. Then the fever comes, and spots on the skin."

"Is it a poison? Could it be the water, like on the Indies?"

"No. It's measles."

"Measles! But the natives say it is a new plague."

"It is new for them," the doctor replied. "We have

233

a name for it; they'll find their own name, I suppose. Mistress Archard's baby is ailing, and young John Sampson. Mistress Dare complains of soreness in her throat."

"What will you do?"

"Not much," the doctor grunted. "Those who have good, well-balanced body humors will get well. Those who don't—will die."

I stepped out into the darkness. The wind whipped at my cloak, and I shivered. From the doorway I saw a beam of light, and the doctor called out after me, "It's like lightning, you know."

I whirled around. "What is?"

"The sickness," he replied. "It never strikes twice in the same place. If you've had it before, you won't get it again."

Measles—little pox, red pox—measles, the killer. I'd had it as a little child and nearly died. I'd had it, and I was safe! But Telana—I wanted only to see her, to be with her everyday. I loved her! I longed for the next day to see her again.

We had three days together. Then the brass bell began to ring. It rang for death.

SEVENTEEN

TELANA HAD HEARD the brass bell. She met me on the path. "What is it, William?"

"The plague," I replied. "It's come here, too. Our bell is like your chant of death."

Her lips framed the word inaudibly, "Who?"

"The son of my friend, Johnny Sampson."

"Oh, William." She drew close; her arms comforted me.

"The baby died, too. Mistress Archard's baby."

We walked out to the grove of pine and cedar. I wanted only to be alone with Telana, away from the hard and anguished faces of my people, away from the moaning funeral chants of the Indians. It was too incredible, almost grotesque, that my heart should be filled with such love, my body with such yearning, when all around me there was death.

"Telana," I told her, looking long into her

eyes, "you must leave Roanoke."

"Leave? Leave you?"

"Yes, until the plague is over."

"But I am well, William!" she cried.

"It moves quickly—*I know*, Telana. It can strike you, too, if you stay here."

"It will not!" she protested. "I do *not* go away from you. You will protect me."

"Has Harawok made even you believe his stories? I can't protect you from this sickness. Don't you think I'd give anything to keep you here near me? Telana, don't you trust me?"

"Yes," she whispered, "but don't send me away."

"You must go," I said firmly. "Go to Croatoan. I'll send for you when it is safe."

She only looked at me, but with such sorrow that I thought I'd weaken. "I want to marry you, Telana," I told her. "I want to take you with me to Chesapeake in the spring. Will you? . . ."

"Yes!" she said. "Oh, yes."

"Isn't it the way of your people, too," I asked sternly, "that a wife obeys her husband?"

She nodded.

"Then obey me now. You'll leave for Croatoan today. Go back to the village and tell your cousin Tequinon that he must take you quickly to Croatoan. And when you see Manteo tell him . . . tell him about us."

"I will tell him," she said meekly, smiling.

"When it's safe, I'll send a messenger for you. Go *now!*" I put out my hand to push her away, but instead I held her fiercely close to me for a long moment, then whispered my goodbye.

I knew afterward it was the right thing to have done, but every day, as the bell rang out again for death, I wished Telana were with me to help me bear it. The bell rang for little Ambrose Viccars, then for his playmate, Bobby Ellis. And Tom Humphrey wandered around the fort like a poor lost soul. He had nobody to play with anymore.

And not only the children died—the bell tolled for Brooke, the shoemaker, for Berde, the farmer, for James Hynde, the thief, and it rang for Agnes Wood.

It was my task to help build the coffins. And each day there were repairs to be made on our dwellings, posts to mend and boards to patch, for now the fierce winds had begun to blow from the Cape, and the clapping of shingles in the night added their dismal sound to my loneliness.

I, who had always enjoyed solitude, did not want to be alone anymore. In the evenings I often sat in the Dare house where some of the men gathered, just so that I might hear the sound of human voices. In all of us, I think, there was this need to drown out the terrible fear we felt, fear for our missing countrymen, fear of sickness, fear of the brass bell sounding again in the morning to tell us that in the night another friend had died.

I would sit by the fire and carve, or go into a corner to sketch. And often it grew late, so that I slept there by the fire, for my own small house seemed suddenly too empty.

Very late one night I sat all alone, sketching, after the others had gone to sleep. Again I had been attempting to sketch Telana, this time from memory. I was so absorbed in my task that the sound of footsteps startled me unreasonably. I leaped up, instinctively hiding the sketch against my chest.

It was Elizabeth, looking pale and drawn.

"I couldn't sleep," she said. "What are you doing?"

"Just sketching," I replied, knowing that she had seen.

"May I see it?"

"It's no good."

"Sketch me!" she said suddenly. "I'll sit for you."

"I can't draw people very well," I said.

"You mean you can't draw me," she snapped. "You can only draw savages! "

"Elizabeth, *please*—I'm tired."

"Let me see that!" she cried, grasping at the sketch. "It's Telana, isn't it? You're in love with her," she said accusingly. "Did you think you could keep it a secret? Is that why you sent her away?"

"I sent her away because of the sickness."

"Then she's coming back?"

"Yes, when I send for her. Elizabeth, I'm not accountable to *you*."

"She'll live with you?"

"She'll be my wife."

She faced me, her features rigid, and I thought

how haggard she was, and how ghostly pale in the dim light. "What is it you're after?" she cried. "What honor? You already sit in with the Assistants. Will the savages make you a chief? Do they pray to you? Are you a god?"

"Elizabeth!"

"You're to build the church at Chesapeake. Soon they'll call you Master. . . ."

"I'll still build the church. Having an Indian wife won't change any of that."

"Oh, won't it?" she cried. "Do you mean you'll still be the same when you're married to a savage? William, for God's sake!"

"Of course I'll be different!" I retorted. "Aren't you different now than when I found you? Aren't we all?"

"No! The rest of us are still civilized, still English, and proud of it. But you—you sit on the floor to eat. You lie on the floor to sleep. And you go running after that half-naked savage girl like a . . . it's disgusting! You can't change yourself, William. You're English. You're *white!*"

"Telana has white blood, too!" I shouted. And instantly I was appalled at my own words.

"I love her!" I cried out. "What do you think I see when I look at her? The color of her skin? It's beautiful! I'll tell you. I see the whole New World in Telana. I see everything that's good and gentle, and I pray to God I'll be worthy of her."

"Worthy!" She flung the word at me, and then she fled.

I was trembling, sick with grief and anger and longing for Telana. I'd go anywhere with her! I'd leave them all, these stupid, blind, dirty-minded people who called themselves civilized and made something ugly and hateful out of my love for Telana.

I realized, upon hearing soft footsteps, that I had slept. The fire was nearly gone. "I still can't sleep," Elizabeth whispered.

Stiffly I got up and threw another log into the embers.

"I'm sorry," she whispered, and held out her hand. "I don't want you to hate me. I didn't want to be so—horrible."

"It's all right."

"Because I've loved you!"

"Elizabeth!"

"I never had anybody to love before you came. And that night—you know, that night of Manteo's christening, I'd made Emme Merrimoth give me a potion." She spoke quickly, breathlessly, without looking at me. "I drank it all. She promised it would work—and Elinor gave me a new dress, and I'd brushed my hair—she *promised!* And then you—you danced with Telana, but Clement danced with me! It worked on Clement, not you!"

"How can anyone be so foolish?" I took her hand, smiling at the memory of that night. "I guess I'm to blame. But you *needed* looking after."

"I loved you from that very first day. And now—you say you want to be *worthy* of Telana. Clement said the same to me, you know. When he left with the others, he kissed me. And he said he was going for me. He wanted to prove himself worthy—of *me*. I could have told him not to go," she said bitterly. "Why didn't I tell him? He didn't have to prove anything for me. But I didn't say anything. I just let him go. I didn't even wish him luck. So," she drew a deep breath, "I'll say it to you. I want you to have—happiness."

"Thank you, Elizabeth."

She moved away from me. "You know," she said, "they won't come back."

"Of course they will!"

"Henry Rufoote says the whole expedition was ill fated from the start."

"Rufoote's always gloomy."

"He says they've been killed."

"Listen, Elizabeth," I said firmly. "Clement wanted to go. Nothing you could have said would have made any difference. He wanted to go, to be with Hugh. Maybe they got to Chesapeake. Maybe they'll be there waiting for us. They might be better off than we are."

She nodded and tried to smile. "It's that awful bell. I hate it. I always think that next time it will be for me."

*   *   *

For days Elizabeth's words rang in my head. "You can't change yourself, William!" and then, "I wish you happiness."

If I were not free to change myself in the

241

direction I wanted to go, how could I ever be happy?

This was the root of my discontent. I had changed. And my people were still the same. They had come halfway across the world, into a land they *knew* would be different. Well then, they would change the land and all the people in it!

I knew now why those afternoons in the Indian village held such peace for me. I could walk among brown-skinned people who saw my ways as strange and even comical. But they accepted me. They never thought to change me.

Everything I had learned from the natives had been at my own request. Never had they forced me to choose, or even called one way better than another. "It is good," they said. Anything that served its purpose was good.

And the purpose, too was clear. To live within the great design that holds all things. To love that which is beautiful and free. To take only that which nature gives willingly. To respect the man, the bear, the deer, equally. To know and to believe that all things pass—the good and the bad—and never to curse the gods for evil.

"It is good," I thought, and was astonished when I realized that in my mind I had used the Indian phrase.

* * *

By the end of December there were eighteen graves on the hillside. The plague of measles had passed. I sent for Telana and Manteo, and they came.

Having Telana made life bearable—even joyful, although the brass bell still sounded for death.

Death came from fevers and dysentery. It came from wounds that wouldn't heal. It came from weakness—many were just not strong enough to endure this harsh land in winter. Most of us were townspeople. We had no idea how to live off the land.

The natives are used to winter. They provide against it. But even so, the food never lasts the whole season. It is a stark fact that in winter they will grow hungry, and some of them will die. But they have had generations of practice in survival. We were totally unprepared and unfit. And besides, many of our stores had been destroyed.

The natives know countless ways of fishing. We had no nets and no hooks. The weirs that the natives had made for us were long since broken. We didn't know how to repair them. Nor did we know how to spear the fish as they did. And we lacked the endurance to sit beside a frozen pond for hours, in the hope that a fish might show.

As for game—it's true that in the deep snow one could track a rabbit. But a rabbit's a meal for one or two, and without enough gunpowder to spend, we were helpless. We tried trapping and failed miserably. There is an art to all things. We were beginners.

I did hunt with my bow and arrow, and I cursed the stubbornness of my fellow colonists who refused to learn. They did not want to stray far from the safety of the fort. And they scorned the "savage" method. Occasionally I shot a deer, and I shared my kill as was expected. But there was never enough. Even the animals knew more about winter than we. Wisely, they slept in secret lairs the whole season long. And they were well hidden.

We grubbed for roots. We roasted lizards. We butchered our horses and ate them. Still, we were hungry. We had very little left to trade with the natives, and they had very little time to help us, because a new plague had struck. Rats.

Rats had infested the granary of the natives, consuming the grain and even attacking the beams and bark of the granary. Then came another wave of sickness.

Over the shrill whistling wind we heard the constant muffled chorus of native drums. "It is a sacrifice," Manteo explained.

"What is there left to sacrifice?" I cried.

"We give to the gods," Telana told me simply.

"Harawok says we have displeased the gods," Manteo said. "The gods have punished us with this plague of rats."

"How does Harawok say you have offended the gods?" I asked.

Stubbornly Manteo replied, "It does not matter."

* * *

I could see the change in Elinor Dare more than in any of the others. The attack of measles had taken all her energy. Dr. Jones said the fever had touched her lungs. No amount of bloodletting or sassafras tea or herbs seemed to help. And Elinor's weakness affected the baby.

"She's starving!" Elizabeth cried. "We've tried to feed her gruel, but she's too little to drink from a cup. I've tried to soak a bit of cloth with soup, but," she shook her head, "she needs milk—mother's milk, and Elinor. . . ."

Whenever I passed the Dare house I would hear Virginia whimpering. At last Elinor Dare asked me to fetch Telana.

Telana came immediately. As she walked toward the Dare house, it was as if everyone along the way had been suddenly struck blind. Nobody nodded, nobody spoke; they all averted their eyes. Proudly, silently, Telana kept on walking, her face passive. But I knew her now and could see beyond the mask to her hurt.

When she saw little Virginia, Telana ran to her, exclaiming, *"Ayee,* poor little one, she is hungry!"

"Telana," said Elinor, "is there a woman among the—among your people who could feed my baby?"

Telana pondered. "It is what she needs—yes, a mother's milk. Oh, yes! Quinsha my friend grieves over her dead baby. Her breasts are full, and there is no little one to drink! So many, many babies have died."

"Would she come?" Elinor asked. "She is the wife of a chief, isn't she? I mean—would she do this?"

"If you ask," said Telana, "she will come. It is honor—and good—to give this gift of life. Perhaps it was the will of the gods that Quinsha stayed here on Roanoke and did not go back to Chawanook. I will bring her to you."

Thus Quinsha came to live at the Dare house, and little Virginia grew strong again. With Virginia thriving, the Dare house became like a haven, quite apart from the rest of the settlement. Inside, the two mothers were content with loving the baby and seeing her grow. Outside, the tongues clucked and wagged, and from house to house the gossip flew.

"Nursed by a savage! Agnes Wood, Lord rest her soul, would turn over in her grave if she knew."

"What virtue can a child absorb from a savage?"

"I tell you, they're getting too high and mighty, coming and going as they please-you'd think Master Dare would keep a firm hand on his own household, at least."

Quinsha stayed for two months, until winter was nearly over. Abruptly she decided to leave for Croatoan.

"She says she must go help her sister with spring planting," Telana told me, "but planting is still far away. Quinsha does not say what is in her heart. She grows to love the baby too much. It is not good to love too much the child of another woman. So Quinsha must go."

* * *

Now I could understand what John Sampson had meant when he said, "It's winter that tests a man." The March winds blew fiercely, reminding us that winter was not yet over. But we carried ourselves with a new sort of pride—we who had been tested and had survived. Death was done with us, we thought.

When the bell rang out one evening, we ran toward the sound in utter disbelief and despair.

Our sentinels stood poised, guns pointed at the shadows as a man slowly crawled into the road. In the darkness he was unrecognizable. Then we heard the cry. "My God! It's a white man!"

His clothes hung in rags and strips about his bony frame. His skin seemed to have been stretched tight across his skull, leaving him like a wild-eyed skeleton, and this creature crawled toward us, raving and calling in sounds without words. By candlelight we saw his face, and in my shock I was only dimly aware of Elizabeth's screaming. It was Clement Taylor, but we knew little joy in the reunion.

Of the thirty-four Englishmen and eight native guides who had left, only nine persons returned. Three of them were natives. We gathered in our survivors, and it was several days before they could tell us the full extent of the massacre.

Yes, they had traveled to Dasamonquepeuk, then north toward Chesapeake. After many weeks of wandering, they found themselves deep in the territory of the Weapemeoc. The Weapemeoc greeted our men with signs of friendship and rejoicing. They prepared a feast and promised to give them guides to Chesapeake.

It was the old treachery reenacted. While our men were feasting, the warriors encircled the camp. With a cry, Wanchese and his men attacked, joined by the best fighters of the Weapemeoc. There was no real battle, only slaughter.

For two days the questioning continued, until our survivors gained the strength to tell it all. Half our men had been killed instantly. The others fled and were ambushed, most of them killed.

Richard Berry—shot in the neck with an arrow.

John Sampson—wooden clubs.

Dyonis Harvie—spears.

A dozen or so of our men hid in the forest, making their way slowly southward with the three guides. Six of them died along the trek from wounds. The others lived on pine nuts and roots, and once they had had the good fortune to kill a wolf. The three remaining native scouts, sick from their wounds, weak from starvation, wandered far in confusion.

Each name of a friend or relative was spoken—then the reply, the anguish, the disbelief. I stood over Clement, asking for Hugh. Was he perhaps only missing? And if he'd died, had it been quick for him, and merciful?

Slowly the story came out. Hugh had been sitting around the fire, laughing and singing. He had put off his sword, and it lay beside him. Hearing the first cry, he had leaped up, thinking it was the call for the dance. The savage nearest him picked up the sword and, wielding it like a cudgel, split Hugh's head in two.

The fate of the women was told in a single word. Captive.

* * *

One hundred fourteen of us had come to the New World. Less than half remained. And one of these was Christopher Cooper.

For a week or so, while the survivors gained their strength, it was only, "Thank God we are alive." Then the old fever for treasure and battle returned, stronger than ever, and it was fed by Chris Cooper and his tales.

They had, of course, failed to reach Chesapeake, but the lure of it was even stronger, for Cooper had come back with a token.

I took these from a little squaw," he would say to his eager listeners, "who got them from a chief of Chesapeake." Again he would hold up the long rope of gleaming white pearls. "Just a sample," he'd say, "compared to what's left."

"Tell it! Tell it again!" the men would urge him, and Cooper would comply.

"Well, not being one to linger over my food, I stole away during the feasting, and I found myself the sweetest little savage wench, just waiting for me in her hut."

"But the pearls! How did you get the pearls?"

"Why, they were lying around her neck, and when she—ah, she was most cordial—'twas as easy as taking sweets from a babe."

"But did she tell you where she got them?"

"Why, from this chief at Chesapeake!"

They counted the weeks. When was the soonest our supply ships might possibly set sail? Then, how long until they anchored here? "We'll have ships and powder and cannon!" Cooper exclaimed. "We'll settle in at Chesapeake, then go back to give those savages a taste of white man's revenge."

Plans for action, treasure and revenge, satisfied them only for a little while. Nearly everyone had suffered the loss of a friend or relative, and vengeance postponed too long loses its sweetness. Thus talk turned into suspicion, and anger turned to a closer target, the natives of Roanoke Island.

"No sooner rested, than they're ready for battle again!" Elizabeth told me incredulously. "Every night the men come to Master Dare's house, hounding him with plans. They're saying that Wanchese had to have help from the Roanoke natives, who knew our soldiers were on the march."

"I've heard them," I said. "They even suspect Manteo. Thank God Manteo stayed here—they'd have said he led them into the trap."

Elizabeth frowned. "William, how could Wanchese possibly have known which way our men were headed, unless some of the Roanoke natives got word to him?"

"Wanchese isn't stupid," I snapped. "He knew when he attacked the storehouse that we'd come after him. He probably counted on it."

"But how could he know which way our soldiers would go?"

"Oh, Elizabeth, we might as well have drawn him a map! He knew how desperately we wanted to get to Chesapeake. Lane risked everything to get there.

And we're just the same. Wanchese *knew* we'd use this chance to go treasure hunting. Richard Berry knew! He knew the men wouldn't be able to resist the temptation. Why, the moment Manteo even hinted that Wanchese might head for Chesapeake, it was all decided."

"But it's possible," Elizabeth persisted, "possible that some of the Roanoke natives did. . . ."

"Possible," I admitted, "but I doubt it. Wanchese is clever. If we'd only realize that, we'd stop thinking this wooden wall will keep our enemies out. Manteo warned us to send scouts ahead, but nobody would listen."

"Well then," she challenged, "what would you have us do?"

"I don't know," I sighed. "Just pray that our ships will come soon."

But it was long before that could happen. Even with the best of luck we'd have to wait another three months. And the next day, when I met with Manteo, I began to realize that time was running out.

EIGHTEEN

MANTEO MADE A LOW, birdlike signal call, deep in his throat. That call and its meaning brought the same emptiness and sorrow I'd known after my father died. For Manteo would not enter our fort anymore; he waited for me outside, crouched low.

"I must speak with you," he said. His face was rigid, but I could see sorrow in his eyes, too.

"You know there is trouble," he continued as we made our way to the grove.

I nodded. "I need to talk to you, too. Some of our men are saying that we were betrayed by your people."

Manteo held up his hand. "You hear the drums. They are restless and angry. Harawok is telling the people that the white man is the cause of plague and death and hunger. He says that the white man caused the rats to eat our grain."

Unable to meet his eyes, I responded, "Some of the colonists say that you have enough grain to share with us, but that your people want us to starve."

As we sat together on the pine needles, sheltered by the thick boughs, I felt closer to Manteo even than when we had hunted together, and he had been my teacher.

"We are the same, you and I," he said at last.

"Yes."

Our presence here in the grove that divided our two villages said it all.

"I tell you," Manteo began, spreading his hands, and I thought for an instant how "white" that gesture was. And as I listened soberly, I wondered how "native" my passive expression might seem.

"Harawok always believed that the white men were gods," Manteo began. "It was he who first told me the legend of Wokokon. It is hard for him to believe that he has been wrong."

"But if he thinks we're gods, then how can he talk against us?" I exclaimed.

"He says we were tricked. It is not unusual for a demon to pretend to be a god, and to fool even a priest. Now Harawok says that the white men are really demons who came masked as gods. And this treachery, he says, is the worst evil."

I asked Manteo, "How does Harawok explain the fact that so many of us have died from plague and wounds?"

"Devils change in shape," Manteo replied. "They

seem to die, but then they reappear in different shape. They must be driven away again and again in all their forms."

"He's got an answer for everything! With explanations like that, what's left for us? Harawok hates us, saying we're devils. Wanchese hates us because we're men, and white. What's the difference? Both of them want to kill us."

"No difference," Manteo said softly.

We looked at each other, and Manteo nodded, as if I'd voiced the question. "It could be," he said, "that Harawok will try to ally with Wanchese."

"Manteo—I must know this. Did Harawok or any of the Roanoke people send word to Wanchese of our soldiers' coming?"

"I do not know," he said. "It could be—it is possible, and I would not hear about it. Harawok and his followers say I have become like the white man, the devil white man."

He stood up. "William, you must talk to your people. You must tell them to leave Roanoke."

"Who would listen to me?" I cried. "They think I'm—oh, they don't say anything, but I can see it in their faces. They hate me for loving Telana, and for having this friendship with you."

"No," Manteo said. "They fear you, because they need you, and you do not need them."

As I walked toward Ananais' house I pondered—not need them? But they were part of me! I wanted their friendship, but I had tasted the New World. I needed it, wanted it, Telana, Manteo, the wilderness and most of all the New World way of looking at life.

It was my choice now. "Do not vacillate!" Rufoote had warned me, and he was right. "Follow your goal!" Ah, Rufoote and Prat and all the others—what could they possibly know about my goals? It was my choice; I need not let myself be divided up into little pieces ever again. I could never take Telana with us. And without her, there was nothing for me at Chesapeake.

But I thought again of the words my mother had combined so long ago when she spoke to me about heaven. Love. Duty. I knocked loudly at Ananais' door.

I told him, simply as I could, what Manteo had said.

"Leave Roanoke?" He stared at me. "Just leave? William, are you mad? It can't be done!"

"We could take the pinnace and sail to one of the islands."

"We must leave the pinnace in the harbor," he exclaimed, pacing in agitation. "It's all we've got left in case something goes wrong."

"It has gone wrong!" I cried. "Harawok knows our powder is nearly gone. Manteo says he might ally with Wanchese."

"And how does Manteo know so much about Wanchese's movements?" Ananais demanded, slamming his fist down on the table.

An earthenware jar fell to the floor and smashed into pieces. From the other room came a deep, racking cough, then Elinor, steadying herself against the doorway pleaded, "Ananais! Don't take on. You'll make yourself ill."

She bent to pick up the broken bits, and her husband shouted, "Leave that alone!"

I struggled to keep my voice calm. "Sir, even Governor White said that if we were in danger, we ought to move."

"Governor White said the Assistants will decide!" Ananais shouted. He sighed, dropped down into the chair, frowning.

"Yes, I could call them together." He withdrew into thought, and Elinor gazed at me, shaking her head slightly.

"Prat—Prat," Ananais murmured, "he won't go. He thinks we're destined to wait here our full span of forty years. And Stevens with his mead and his memoirs."

"If you were to propose it, Ananais," Elinor said softly, "the people might be willing. If you explain . . ."

"Explain what? We have no proof of anything."

"But William has told you. . . ."

"Yes! He's said we must abandon our colony! Let him take his savage wench then and hide in the wilderness. That's really what you want, isn't it?" he shouted, glaring.

"Ananais, that's unfair," murmured Elinor.

"And what will they say of me if I lead our people away from here, from the protection of our fort, and lead them into an ambush? How do we know Wanchese isn't just waiting for us on one of those islands? And when our supply ships come and find us gone, what will they say of me, except that I hadn't the courage to hold this land. And do I leave someone here, as Grenville did, to be slaughtered? Will they say of me, as they say about Governor Lane, that I ran off at the first sign of trouble?"

"How could they?" I protested. "We've held this fort all winter, all through the sickness and plague . . ."

"Yes! And then to give it all up, because of the rumors of a savage who might just as well be in league with Wanchese!"

"But he isn't," I cried. "He's our friend."

Ananais turned toward me, and with fists clenched he said with heavy loathing, "*We* have no friends among the savages."

I strode out, slamming the door behind me. But I had not gone far when I heard my name called, and Elinor came hurrying toward me. "William! He didn't mean those things. He's overburdened—it's hard, so *hard* to know what's best. And whom can he ask? Chris Cooper would march out in a moment, even with this army of skeletons. If only he could counsel with reasonable men! They're all gone, Sampson and Howe . . . day after day people come to Ananais for reassurance. And he must tell them, 'Yes, yes, our ships are on the way. There's nothing more to fear now.' Oh, William, Ananais is a good man, and my husband, so perhaps it's wrong of me to say this. But he was never meant to govern alone."

"Perhaps you can persuade him," I said. "We

never planned to settle here from the start. It isn't important that we hold Roanoke. We can wait some other place for our ships."

"I cannot sway him," she said, suppressing a cough. "It's partly because of me, I think, that he will not leave Roanoke."

"Because of *you?*"

"We're tired, William, all of us. But I—I am more tired than the others. I couldn't endure the journey."

"To Croatoan or Wokokon? Of course you could."

"No, not even to Croatoan. It's not only the journey, but everything connected with it. And even if Ananais proposed it, I don't think the people would move. We have given too much . . ." She sighed, gazing over the hills. "I would like to see Chesapeake, she murmured. "I think it must be very beautiful."

"You will," I said, but my voice sounded hollow. "Maybe Ananais is right. Probably our ships have already set sail, and with good weather. . . ."

"But I have seen more this year," she continued dreamily, "than most people would in a lifetime. And I have given Ananais a child—and she *is* lovely, isn't she? Strong and healthy—I know what they said about Quinsha, but it was all nonsense. She's a beautiful child. William!" Suddenly she grasped my sleeve. "After I am—William! If something should happen to Ananais, who will look after Virginia? Will you?" she pleaded. "Will you?"

Her eyes had the intense glow of a person seeing a vision. Her frail body was bent toward me, entreating. I could only stare at her, mouthing objections, lies. "Nothing will happen, you'll see."

"Promise me, William, if you can, look after her. Say it. 'Elinor, I will look after Virginia.'"

"Elinor," I said, "I will look after Virginia. Of course I will—need you ask? I'm her godfather."

She thanked me and smiled her brilliant smile, then lightly she began to talk about good times in the past and good times to come.

And as I watched her face and listened to her voice, I felt suddenly flooded with love—love for my people. I seemed to see them all before me, even those now dead, all together in their weaknesses, their damnable stubbornness, their pride and foolishness—and their courage. Yes, I would leave them. But a part of what they were would always go with me. I prayed that it would, as I prayed for strength to keep my promises.

* * *

We buried Elinor Dare on the shaded knoll with the others. It was late in March, a mild, lovely day with a blue sky and the first hint of greenery.

Elizabeth wept as if her heart would break. "William, I can't bear it. Truly, I can't."

"You can," I told her. "You will. You've got to look after Virginia now."

She devoted herself entirely to the child, and to keeping house for Ananais. And strangely, Ananais began to speak about Roanoke as if he would never leave it. As soon as the frost was over, he said, we would begin planting. Nobody could talk to him anymore about Chesapeake, or about the ships that must come with relief.

But I began to think only of the ships. Endlessly I spoke to Telana about Bessie, how we would show Bessie the New World together.

But Telana only listened, and I felt that beyond my voice she was straining to listen to the drums. I called them winter drums, drums of death, of mourning. Since the first plague of measles, they had not stopped, but they beat a steady accompaniment to every changing thought.

One day the drums suddenly stopped. I ran straight to the village to find Telana, joyful at the silence. It could only mean that the natives, too, were finished with mourning and sacrifice.

I found Telana, embraced her, exclaiming, "Oh, Telana! The drums have stopped. Now I know winter's over. They're talking of planting, and soon. . . ."

I felt the stiffness in her arms. She turned her face away from me.

"What's wrong, my love? What is it?" I sat down on the mat beside her, and she whispered, "The silent drums do not mean what you think." She half smiled at me, the way a mother smiles at the foolishness of her child, but with love. "William," she said, "now I tell you. You must leave Roanoke."

"But the drums . . ." I began.

"Harawok has called the people for conference. Not all, but many will listen to him. The people listen to a priest."

"But a conference could mean anything," I objected. "It could mean he wants to make peace with us."

"It could mean he has thought of a way to—to kill the white man. It could mean he has sent for Wanchese. First he talks with chiefs. Then for many days chiefs will talk and think. But not *very* many days. You must go now! Make yourselves ready now and *go.*"

"They won't go," I told her. "I've already talked to Ananais, and I've told you."

"They will wait for attack?"

"Ananais won't go, and without him none of the others will either."

"Then you," she said breathlessly, "you and I will go. Manteo will take us. We will be on Croatoan by tonight."

She took my hand, pulled me upright. "Come. You come with me to Croatoan. We have many friends on Croatoan. Nobody would harm you. So come! Make ready."

I looked at her for a long moment, thinking only of her beauty, slowly shaking my head.

"What? Is it the ships?" she cried. "Your ships from across the sea might pass Croatoan even before they reach Roanoke. You will see them."

"Telana. . . ." I held her close.

"Come now! William, if you die—I die too. Yes, I will."

"Telana, listen to me. You must wait for me a little longer. I can't leave my people now. I wouldn't leave you if you were in danger."

261

"William, there is so much for us to do together! I want to show you Secota, where I was born. With you I will see it again, new."

"We'll go to Secota, I promise you. After our ships come, after Bessie comes, we'll be married and live together. And I have decided, Telana, that we will not live in the colony."

I saw her quick look of surprise and joy. "William! You give me everything, but then you say I must wait! Why do we wait? Your people," she said heatedly, "always wait and wait, until time is all gone into the little box."

"It would be wrong for me to go with you now," I said firmly. "I'd wonder later, and so would you, whether I came away with you just to save myself, or because I truly chose it. I must stay, and I know you understand. Duty is the same for all people." I smiled slightly, thinking that someday I would tell Telana about my childish question and my mother's reply. But now I only held Telana close and kissed her, thinking, yes, it's these two things that make us human—duty and love.

"William," she whispered, "you cannot help them."

"I have to try once more. I'll think of a way. I'll talk to Ananais tomorrow."

I found Manteo, and together we made a plan that would force Ananais to move. Tomorrow Manteo would go to Croatoan. He would return the same afternoon, with two or three of the chiefs. The chiefs would invite our settlers to their island. It would all be done in the most natural way. Manteo would insist that we must go—it would be an insult to refuse.

I could imagine it all now, Manteo speaking gravely, "You come to Croatoan for planting festival. All come—women and children, too. Stay seven days."

Seven days would be long enough for Manteo's trusted scouts to discover Harawok's plan. It would be long enough for Manteo to send a message to Menantenon, his father, to send warriors to our aid.

As soon as we were out of danger, I would tell Ananais my decision to leave the colony and live with Telana and her people. I had worried about Bessie. Would she be willing to come with us? Yes, I decided; she was young and not set in her ways. She would understand my choice and agree.

Tomorrow, I thought, reenacting my plans as I lay down to sleep. Tomorrow marked the beginning. Tomorrow, by sunset, we'd be on our way to Croatoan, Telana and I. . . .

NINETEEN

IN THAT MOMENT of shock, I thought that some violent dream had awakened me. I recognized only the pounding of my heart. Then I realized that the violence was not inside me, but in the throbbing of the bell, in the screams of men and women, in the sound of roaring flames, in the bitter smell of smoke.

In panic, I ran, grasping as I went for something familiar—I did not even think what it was. Flames licked at the back wall of my own small house, and I stepped out into higher flames and an agony of destruction. I saw a man fleeing, his nightshirt a mass of flames. I saw another with blood streaming from his mouth and eyes. A roof gave way, sending a burst of sparks around me. I saw Emme Merrimoth swinging a club, holding a gleaming dark attacker at bay—but only for a moment and then she was down. I saw Henry Rufoote clutching a musket in both hands. I saw Christopher Cooper huddled under the silent cannon, his lips working mutely.

The wall was a mass of flames, and from outside I heard the cries of the attackers. "White devils! White devils will die tonight!"

Again we had misjudged Wanchese, how he would seize this moment, how he would use our own wooden wall and make it our funeral pyre.

"White devils! White devils.will die tonight!"

Like animals caught in an ambush, we were without choice. Instinct alone controlled us; some froze, some ran. With the others I ran toward the gate.

But out of the chaos I felt an iron grip on my arm, and I heard a voice close to my ear, "*This* way!"

Still I resisted, blindly pressing forward with the others. "This way!" Manteo's hands pulled me away from the crowd and the clanging bell. He half dragged me to the far wall, which the flames had not yet reached.

"Climb onto my shoulders!"

I obeyed and jumped to the other side. A moment later Manteo dropped down beside me; he pushed me down low among the bushes.

"Where's Telana?"

"By the water—there." He motioned toward the jagged plateau where Telana and I had stood—it seemed so long ago. "She is waiting," he said, "with a canoe. We'll climb—down—to her."

The cliff seemed miles and miles away, with everything in between larger than life. Life itself seemed far, far away, and with death so near, seemed almost undesired.

"White devils!"

A great roar came, and I knew the gate had crumbled, that those beneath it had been alive just a moment ago, and I had been with them.

"Elizabeth!" I cried.

"I saw her go out. She has the baby. Stay down!" Manteo commanded. "I'll find her."

We found Elizabeth crouched among the trees near the beach where we had landed. She had dropped, exhausted, holding Virginia close, shielding her with her body.

"The pinnace," she gasped, and then, "Clement! Ananais! Wait for them!"

Manteo half lifted her. "No. There—Telana waits."

I tried to take the baby from her, but Elizabeth screamed and even cursed, refusing to move until she held the child once more.

Half dragging Elizabeth, we made our way through the trees, making a wide arc around the burning fort. All gunshots had stopped, leaving only the beating of drums, the shouts of the warriors, "White devils will die tonight!"

An arrow flew past and landed at my feet. Instantly Manteo turned, set his arrow toward the tree top, and I heard the heavy thud of a body falling to the ground.

We made our way up the hill, half crouching, and now I realized what it was I had clutched in that terrible moment. It was the bow Manteo had made for me—my bow which I kept beside my bed.

The jagged rocks cut into our feet. The incline became steeper, our breathing heavier. Now Manteo took the baby, slung her into the bosom of his cloak, and I reached down to pull Elizabeth up onto the rocks. My own voice was harsh and rasping, "Hurry. Hurry." Below I heard the sounds of pursuit. Just three or four more footholds, and we would reach the top of the ledge, then down the cliffs to the water where Telana waited.

"Elizabeth," I called, grasping her hand. "We're nearly there." Her hand slipped from mine. "Give me your hand."

Then I heard the whirr of an arrow and her small outcry of surprise. Elizabeth slid down into the darkness. As her body fell backward, I saw that the arrow had pierced her chest. I kept reaching down with my hand, part of me knowing that she was dead, but part of me refusing to know, still reaching down into the darkness. I felt the strange sensation of being away and apart from it all, my senses floating free. I felt the wetness of tears on my face, flowing, flowing apart from my thoughts, apart from my movements. My hands moved with a will of their own to place the arrow to the bow. Dimly I saw Manteo beside me, ready to shoot. We were like twin shadows with a single will.

We shot. I don't know how many times, with what strength or accuracy. We shot. We shot at gleaming teeth and white paint, at the flashing

267

whites of their eyes and their bobbing heads. We shot, and in my feverish brain they all passed before me, and it was for them that the arrows flew—for Hugh, for Brooke, for Ambrose Viccars and Joyce Archard and Elinor Dare and George Howe. . . .

"Enough!" Manteo shouted at last. "They are dead."

"How many?"

"Wanchese and two others."

Now I looked to the distance at the white sails of the pinnace spread out like wings. I could see her moving slowly away.

"Come!" Manteo said. "Quickly."

I unsheathed my knife, pressed all my weight against the point of the blade and carved the letter "C" into the one lone tree on the ledge.

"William!" It was Telana's voice. "There is no time!"

Again I pressed the blade—"R."

Below us I heard the crackling of torches. Manteo pulled at my arm, and quickly I carved the letter "O."

We stumbled down the rocks, half sliding. My feet were cut and bleeding. At last I felt the cool water. Manteo took up the paddle. I pushed the canoe into the stream, and we moved out. Strange, I could see it as if I stood above on the cliff, the four of us in the canoe on the water—Manteo, Telana, the baby and I—cut off from everything, moving down the dark, dark water.

We didn't speak. Manteo's muscles rippled as he

rowed, and I matched my strokes to his. As we rowed, I gazed at Telana's face and at the baby sleeping in her arms. Her expression was grave, half stern, half serene. I thought fleetingly of the faces carved into the posts at the ceremonial ground at Croatoan, and I wondered whether my expression was the same. I suppose it was. Even when there is time for mourning, when the funeral wails are loud and terrible, it must be brief. Real suffering remains inside where it cannot show. It must not show, or the depth of their grief would harden a people past compassion.

Compassion shone in Telana's eyes. At last I said to her, using the Indian tongue, "My heart is full."

She nodded, and I watched her as the sun began slowly to rise in a faint fringe of light just over the horizon.

* * *

How many of my countrymen had survived? I couldn't even guess. The only hope was that the pinnace had landed somewhere safely, with however many had gotten aboard.

But after several weeks scouts brought a message to Croatoan. The remains of a strange ship with white sails had been washed onto a northern shore. The timbers were battered and split. The sails were ripped into shreds. Not one person, living or dead, was found.

Manteo sent messengers in every direction. All the tribes sent the same report—no white men, none. Where were they? How could they all have disappeared? It seemed that the land itself had swallowed them up. Brutal and harsh are the demands of the wilderness: it gives no warning, man must change to meet its terms, or he will die.

When we landed on Croatoan, Quinsha had been there to meet our canoe. It was almost as if she had expected us. "The gods willed that I stay," she said. "I was held here to wait." Now she allowed herself to love little Virginia fully.

Telana and I would watch her walking on the beach with Virginia, whose reddish hair gleamed in the sun, contrasting with the Indian mother's darkness. They would sit down on the sand beside Telana and me; together we would scan the waves.

One month after our landing at Croatoan, Telana and I celebrated our marriage feast. On that day we began the ritual of going out to look for the ships. Everyday we looked, and as we watched for the ships, I'd tell Telana again about England and how it would be when Bessie came.

All that summer we waited for the ships. When the leaves began to fall from the trees, we knew. Our ships would not come. It didn't matter why. And, just as they had failed to come this year, they might fail the next year and the next. It was time to settle in before winter. And I had promises to keep.

Our first child would soon be born. I had promised Telana that it would be born at Secota.

It was time for Quinsha to return to her husband at Chawanook. She would take Virginia with her. "The child will be loved," Manteo said. "She will be another child of the legend."

Thus we set out from Croatoan, with Manteo to guide us. He would take Quinsha and Virginia to Chawanook, then return to Croatoan. He would watch for the ships, and would send a message if they arrived. Virginia would then be returned to her people.

Our Croatoan friends came to the beach to sing songs of farewell. They gave us food from their rich harvest. It had been a good year.

On the mainland we left the canoe bound to a sturdy tree and made our way westward on foot. Manteo and I carried Virginia on a litter made of saplings and matting. We walked for six days. On the sixth day Telana told me, "Tomorrow you will see Secota."

We parted. Manteo would go north with Virginia and Quinsha; Telana and I would travel south.

"You will come to Secota," Telana reminded Manteo, "when the snow has melted."

Manteo smiled. "I will come with my gift of welcome for your child."

I picked up little Virginia and held her close, touching her soft curls. "And you must bring Virginia to see me," I said.

Manteo nodded. "Goodbye, my brother," he said, clasping my arms in an embrace.

I watched him go, carrying Virginia on his back.

Telana led me up to a plateau, then she pointed. "Secota," she said, smiling.

I could see the town clearly, the small huts, the

paths and fields all laid out and blended into the green hills. There were no fences around the town of Secota. The land stretched on and on, wooded hills, green valleys, which promised cool lakes and streams, on and on as far as I could see, as far as I could travel in a lifetime.

"The New World," I whispered, taking Telana's hand.

She nodded and moved close to me.

For a moment my thoughts turned back to Bessie, and my promise to her, still unkept. Did she think me dead? Would she sail some day to find me?

Suddenly Telana laughed softly. "The child," she said. "He moves. He wishes to go home, I think."

"Come, then," I said, and we walked toward Secota, and I felt a great sense of peace and the certainty that Bessie would find her own New World, just as I had found mine.

EPILOGUE

THE MAJOR EVENTS portrayed in this story are true; they are a matter of historical record. Thomas Hariot, the historian of the 1585—86 expedition to Virginia published his account of the land and the people. John White's letters and his Journal have been preserved to this day.

Governor White left his colonists on Roanoke Island on August 27, 1587. In letters to his friend, historian Richard Hakluyt, he explained the circumstances that prevented his immediate return to Virginia.

In spring 1588, attack by the Spanish Armada was imminent. Queen Elizabeth forbade the departure of all ships that might be used in the impending battle. But with Sir Walter Raleigh's help, John White secured the necessary funds for two ships and supplies. The supply ships, also carrying fifteen newly recruited colonists, set sail from England on April 22, 1588.

As soon as the ships were on the high seas, the sailors began to search for Spanish treasure. In May, the battle of the Spanish Armada began. The two relief ships were defeated and probably looted in an encounter with a Spanish vessel. They limped home.

By July the Armada had been defeated. But still no relief ships were sent to Virginia all that year and the next. The reason—Raleigh's funds had run out, and no new investors could be found. At last, in February, 1590, John White persuaded the commander of a merchant fleet bound for the Indies to take him aboard. No sooner were the ships loaded, than an order was issued forbidding all ships to leave the ports of England. Through Walter Raleigh, White obtained a release for the ships, with the condition that the commander carry the planters and supplies to Virginia. But the captain refused to carry any passengers or provisions. He would take only John White and his personal belongings. With the ships ready to sail, and no more time to appeal to Raleigh, John White set out for Virginia to seek his countrymen.

Again the sailors went plundering. They spent the spring and summer capturing and engaging Spanish ships near the Indies. It was August 17, 1590, before John White and a searching party set foot on Roanoke Island.

They sounded the trumpet call and played tunes

of familiar English songs. They were met with silence. To their joy they saw a thick column of smoke and ran toward it. It was only a brush fire.

They searched the island and found only torn dwellings and the remains of a palisade overgrown with weeds. On a wooden post they saw the word CROATOAN clearly carved. They walked to the north end of the island. On the crest of a cliff they saw a tree carved with the letters CRO.

John White was overjoyed at finding no sign of distress. He determined to go to Croatoan the following day. A fierce storm broke out. Three anchors were lost. Food and water were giving out. They decided to spend the winter at Porto Rico and take up the search the following spring. But again their plans were defeated. A strong wind blew the ships off their southern course and straight for England. The fleet reached Plymouth on October 24, 1590. It was John White's last voyage.

In a letter to Richard Hakluyt, John White lamented, ". . . I would to God it (the venture) had been as prosperous to everyone as it proved poisonous to the planters, and as joyful to me as it was useless to them. Yet . . . I must remain content . . . I leave off attempting that in which I would to God my wealth would support my will. Thus I commit the relief of my uneasy company of planters in Virginia to the merciful help of the Almighty, whom I most humbly beseech to help and comfort them. . . ."

John White retired to one of Raleigh's estates in

Ireland and was not heard from again. But seventy-five of his watercolor paintings, the first pictorial record of the New World, have survived to this day. They are widely reproduced in history books; a large collection can be seen at the British Museum, or reproduced in Stefan Lorant's book, *The New World*, Duell, Sloan & Pearce, New York, 1946.

In his letters John White revealed that Captain Ferdinando and his crew returned to England sick and weakened, and without the treasure they had hoped to take.

Church records show that in London in the year 1592, Elizabeth Wythers and Robert Taylor were married.

The lost colony of Roanoke has been called one of the greatest unsolved mysteries in American history. One fact continues to haunt those who seek to solve it; in 1607, when English settlers came to plant another colony at Jamestown, they heard rumors of fair-haired "Indians" living in the New World.

Acknowledgments

For historical information, the author is particularly indebted to:

William S. Powell, Librarian of the University of North Carolina, for his personal communications and for his article, "Roanoke Colonists and Explorers; An Attempt at Identification," *North Carolina Historical Review*, April 1957, vol. 34, no. 2. (In this article Mr. Powell tells the background and occupations of many of the Roanoke colonists.)

David Beers Quinn, "The Roanoke Voyages (1584—90)," London: *The Hakluyt Society*, vol. 2, 1955.

Stefan Lorant, *The New World*, Duell, Sloan & Pearce, New York, 1946.